THE VAMPYRE

Retold by David Campton

Based on a story by John Polidori

General Editor: John Halkin

BARRON'S

New York

Also available in the
Fleshcreeper series
BLOOD FROM THE MUMMY'S TOMB
FANGS OF THE WEREWOLF
FRANKENSTEIN
DR. JEKYLL AND MR. HYDE
First edition for the United States and the Philippines
published 1988 by Barron's Educational Series, Inc.

First published 1986 by Hutchinson Children's Books, an
imprint of Century Hutchinson Ltd, London, England.

All inquiries should be addressed to:
Barron's Educational Series, Inc.
250 Wireless Boulevard
Hauppauge, New York 11788

Library of Congress Catalog Card No. 88-15911

International Standard Book No. 0-8120-4070-8

Library of Congress Cataloging-in-Publication Data
Campton, David.
    The vampyre / retold by David Campton.— 1st ed.
       p.   cm.— (Fleshcreepers)
    "Based on a story by John Polidori."
    Summary: A young Englishman traveling on the
Continent with the mysterious Lord Rutven comes to realize
that his companion is an evil and murderous vampire.
    ISBN 0-8120-4070-8
    [1. Vampires—Fiction. 2. Horror stories.] I. Polidori,
John William, 1795-1821. Vampyre. II. Title. III. Title:
Vampire. IV. Series.
PZ7.C16155Vam 1988   88-15911
[Fic]—dc19   CIP
                                                  AC

PRINTED IN THE UNITED STATES OF AMERICA

890 5500 987654321

CONTENTS

A Scream in the Night	3
Lord Ruthven	8
Found Dead	14
Money or Your Life	19
Grand Tour	26
Goodbyes	34
Last Night	40
Letters	45
The Italian Girl	51
Vampire	59
Death in the Woods	68
Death in the Mountains	75
Damning Evidence	89
The Hanging	92
Remember Your Oath	102
After Dark at Vauxhall	110
What Was the Message?	121
Deadly Wedding	127
Ten Hours to Moonrise	131

But first on earth, as vampires sent,
Thy corse shall from the tomb be rent,
Then ghastly haunt thy native place
And suck the blood of all thy race.
                    Lord Byron, *The Giaour*

About this Book

Is there anything worse than a wet vacation when there is nothing to do but stay indoors? Well, this is how the story of the vampire came about.

It was the year after the battle of Waterloo. Four young people were on vacation near Lake Geneva: the poet, Lord Byron, and his physician, John Polidori, together with the poet, Shelley, and his friend Mary, whom he later married.

For a whole week rain poured down. To pass the time they started reading fleshcreeping horror stories. Soon they were tempted to try writing fleshcreepers of their own. Out of that rainy week came Mary Shelley's *Frankenstein* and John Polidori's *The Vampyre,* here retold by David Campton. At least one wet vacation was not such a dead loss after all!

The Vampyre was first published anonymously and the public imagined that Lord Byron himself must be the author. It became immensely successful. Many later authors imitated it, adding their own ideas to the vampire theme, but John Polidori's story was the very first in English.

It begins when Aubrey, a wealthy young man, discovers a murdered girl in the dark streets of early nineteenth-century London . . .

John Halkin

ONE
A Scream in the Night

A scream of terror tore through the dark, for an instant overwhelming the clatter of wheels and horses from London's nighttime traffic. The torch of the boy in front of me flickered even more uncertainly in his shaking hand as he stopped dead.

"'Ear that, sir!"

"Of course I heard." As if in reply, the scream was repeated, not far away in the blackness. A girl was in fear for her life. "Come on, before it's too late."

The boy would not move and I could not—at least not without the feeble glow of his torch. Every window in the street seemed shuttered against the night. With moon and stars blotted out by thick clouds, a man would be running blind. As my old guardian recently warned me, death can lurk anywhere on the streets of London—particularly in shadows.

"This way." I seized the reluctant urchin by the shoulders and pushed him in the direction of the sound. It seemed to come from a nearby side street and, even now, struck a different, more chilling note. Frantic appeal was giving way to cries of almost resigned despair. "Hurry, boy. Hurry!" I shouted. "She could be dead before we find her."

"What you goin' to do about 'er when we does?" he whined.

At that moment I neither knew nor cared. The sound

3

died away with a sobbing moan until I could hear nothing except the boy's whimpering.

"Can't 'ear nothin' now," he whispered hoarsely.

"For pity's sake, listen!"

At the far end of the street, scurrying feet and raised voices accompanied distant flickering as others made their way towards those frantic cries. Doors were opening, throwing beams of light across the cobblestones.

Questions were barked into the gloom.

"Who's that?"

"What's going on there?"

For a few seconds, all beyond the boy and myself was blotted out by what appeared to be a shadow, looming between us and the commotion. I swear I heard a laugh, low and diabolical—almost low enough to have been a figment of my imagination and devilish enough to have strayed from a nightmare. In the space of a couple of heartbeats it was gone.

The boy pressed against me as though for protection.

"What was that?"

Who could say what it was? Pointless to strain my eyes into the darkness after a thing that passed like a rushing cloud.

An excited babble came from the group gathered down the street. Made bolder by company, the boy trotted in front of me towards them. At the prospect of more light to add to their few lanterns, the small huddle parted to let us through.

The light from my guide's torch fell on a slight figure lying face downward on the steps of what appeared to be an unoccupied house. She had wasted precious time beating on an unresponsive door.

A man, a servant by his clothing, turned her over and

4

together the watchers breathed a sigh of pity. The girl could have been no more than sixteen.

Her face was too doll-like to be really pretty, but no girl of her age can be counted plain. Her dress, though not in the height of fashion, was of good quality and not a hand-me-down, either.

A woman began to sob. "Poor thing. What was she doing alone in the street?"

The girl's mouth was slightly open, frozen in the grimace of her last despairing cry. Her eyes were wide, as though still staring at the horror that had just struck her down. Her dress was slightly disarranged, exposing her neck, but aside from that, she showed no signs of violence. How then had she died?

I thought she seemed so pale as to be—bloodless.

The men in the group wearing hats removed them in the presence of death.

"Fetch a policeman," urged someone.

"Fetch a doctor," shouted another.

A portly person, with a cloak hastily pulled over his formal suit, elbowed me aside.

"I *am* a doctor," he boomed. Then, bending over the girl, he pronounced with authority what we already knew. "Life is extinct."

When halted by the fearful cries, I had been hurrying to my apartment, already late for my next engagement. If I stayed any longer, I knew I would be caught up in an affair that did not really concern me. I took the doctor's arm.

"Sir." Given half a chance, he would be asking why this young whippersnapper should buttonhole him. So I assumed as much authority as an independent eighteen-year-old may.

"My name is Aubrey, sir. I live in this neighborhood. My card, sir . . ." I continued to chatter while I fumbled inside my overcoat for the confounded piece of cardboard. "If I can be of further assistance, do not hesitate to call on me. In the meantime—most urgent business—elsewhere . . ."

I thrust the card into his hand. While he squinted at it, trying to read, I walked away with the boy and the light.

There was no need to tell anyone that my urgent appointment was at Lady Mercer's reception. I was late only because I had lingered too long over my boxing lesson at Hartwell's gymnasium.

My apartment was only a few streets further, near Lincoln's Inn Fields. My guardian had rented it for me so that I would be near enough to him in case of trouble, but far enough away not to trouble him. He understood all there was to know about money and absolutely nothing about people—especially young people.

I was thankful for small mercies: for the first time in my young life I was in London, at liberty, with money to spend and a dressing table piled with invitations to balls, parties and gatherings.

Once in my apartment, I sent my tie flying in one direction and my vest in another. Fortunately I did not need to shave more than once a day in order to present an acceptable face to company in the evening. As I washed and changed into a freshly laundered shirt, I was mentally rehearsing the tale I would tell.

No one else at the reception tonight would be able to boast of an encounter with murder. Even now I was looking forward to the admiration I would excite among the ladies. I could almost hear their shocked squeals at each bloodcurdling detail.

I pushed to the back of my mind any reflection that the subject of my story was not a mere broken doll but, a few hours before, had been alive with hopes and ambitions of her own . . .

I never told that story. Lord Ruthven had arrived at the reception before me.

TWO
Lord Ruthven

My first impression of Lord Ruthven was of a shadow against the light of hundreds of candles in the great chandeliers of Mercer House. His black evening clothes and dark hair were in startling contrast to the pallor of his face.

I asked Lady Loveborough by my side who the stranger standing so aloof might be. She made a noise half way between a sniff and a cough—her signal of disapproval. "Ruthven," she said.

"Lord Ruthven? The guest of honor?"

"This evening's freak," she said heavily. "Lady Mercer is never content with mere out-of-season fruit and flowers. We must also be offered something to talk about in the way of a two-headed snake or a dancing bear. Lord Ruthven? Not so much an honored guest as a performing monster. This evening, though, her monster is refusing to perform," she added, with massive satisfaction.

At this moment, across the crowded reception room, Lord Ruthven seemed to be looking directly at me.

"A woman of Lady Mercer's age should know better than to wear a gown of that color," said Lady Loveborough to herself—but loud enough for those near her to hear. "It makes the color of her cheeks look more painted than usual."

Caught by Lord Ruthven's dark stare, I felt impelled to cross the wide expanse of marble floor towards him

"As for all those bracelets," went on Lady Loveborough, now behind me, "the wonder is that she can lift·her arms with the weight of them."

The diamonds now sparkled as Lady Mercer waved her hands. Her voice rose higher and higher in her attempts to capture his lordship's attention.

"Lord Ruthven, may I present my young friend . . ."

He, though, was looking past her as if she did not exist. He seemed to be gazing at me.

Slowly, I made my way forward, passing the silks and jewels of some of the richest women in England without even noticing them. I was hardly aware of anything beyond that pale face.

I thought, "Where have I seen skin so waxen before?" A memory of the dead girl flashed across my mind. Ridiculous! I was thinking too much about her. Certainly Lord Ruthven was no corpse.

"Lord Ruthven!" shrieked Lady Mercer. "I am speaking to you!"

The people nearest her fell silent. The hush spread, until all that could be heard was the music in the nearby ballroom.

At last, Lady Mercer admitted defeat. She retreated from the dark figure, and looked around at the rest of us, gaping. As if caught making some rude gesture, everyone began to chatter.

Lord Ruthven nodded once in my direction, then turned and walked slowly from the hall. The buzz of conversation was stilled around him as he passed, like a path of silence being cut across the floor. So he left.

Lady Loveborough laid a heavy hand on my arm. "Mr. Aubrey, are you bewitched?"

I wanted to say, "Yes. Bewitched is exactly how it feels. As if those eyes could cast a spell." Aloud I merely said, "I am so sorry, Lady Loveborough. But you must agree that Lord Ruthven is a fascinating creature."

Lady Loveborough snorted.

I went on hastily, "He reminds me of my favorite books. Gothic horrors, all graves and goings-on at midnight, with the heroine rescued in the last chapter."

"Books!" Lady Loveborough had little use for them.

"You forget, Lady Loveborough, that when I was a boy, books and my sister were my sole companions. My parents were killed when I was only ten, leaving me in the hands of a governess and tutor. Since I was happiest with my head in a book, they were happy to leave it there."

"Surely you have outgrown that circulating library nonsense by now? I would not even want my Jane to be reading it."

"Miss Loveborough will never lack livelier companions," I assured her. "But, speaking personally, I do hope to meet Lord Ruthven again."

"Most unlikely," declared Lady Loveborough. "After such rudeness towards Lady Mercer—richly though the silly woman deserved it—he will never receive another invitation where invitations matter."

She was wrong.

Everyone was talking about him. Invitations came from Lady Jersey and Lady Oxford. Lord Ruthven was seen at Holland House—after which requests for his company flooded in from all the other society hostesses.

I had my share, too.

My guardian had said, "A young man with good health, good looks, good family and a good fortune had better be on his guard against mamas with unmarried daughters."

In spite of this warning, I accepted most of the

invitations. I wanted to meet Lord Ruthven. Yet Fate seemed to be against all my attempts. Sometimes I would arrive at a party after he had left. Sometimes I would leave before he arrived. At each failure the mystery surrounding him increased.

Although truth was hard to come by, there seemed no end to the gossip.

The Wynter twins, for instance—Amelia and Arabella—knew everything and nothing. One slender, dark and listless, the other plump, fair and playful, they were equally silly and given to outbursts of giggling. They may have been tolerable as companions, but Lady Wynter had something more binding in mind for me. I was always made welcome at their house in Audley Street.

In Lady Wynter's drawing room the twins were gossiping about their favorite topic, Ruthven.

"Those eyes," twittered one. "Dark, dark eyes that look right down into your heart. He knows exactly what you are feeling."

"He wouldn't need to look into my heart," tittered the other. "I would tell him myself. That voice! So low and deep. With that voice he can persuade anyone to do anything."

I inquired if they were talking about me, provoking more giggles, more tinkling of teacups.

"Ruthven, silly." Arabella tossed her fair curls in a way which might have inspired puppy love in a school-boy, but which was lost on me.

"Have you met him?" I asked, perhaps a bit too eagerly.

"No. But we know all about him."

"What do you know?"

"Charlotte Eustace says he must be a hundred years

old," said Amelia. "Her grandmother remembers Lord Ruthven and he was an old man of thirty when she was a girl."

"That may be," I said, rather angrily, feeling that she was trying to make a fool of me. "In time, Lord Ruthven's son would have become Lord Ruthven. Just as *his* son will become the next Lord Ruthven. So there will always be Lord Ruthvens."

"But no one can remember a Ruthven ever being married. One must be married, you know, before one can have a son." Amelia imparted this information as though instructing me in a subject of which I was totally ignorant. As I did not reply, the twins babbled on.

"Ruthven Castle is a ruin."

"And always has been."

"Lord Ruthven was murdered by Jacobins in the French Revolution."

"Lord Ruthven was eaten by wolves in Russia."

"Lord Ruthven was killed in a duel in Prussia."

Each absurdity was accompanied by a gust of girlish laughter until the gust grew into a gale—which was suddenly stilled.

The girls stood speechless as angels on a headstone, all color draining from their cheeks.

Not a sound was heard beyond the chatter and clatter at the far end of the room. With an unhesitating swoop, I saved the Wynter china from being shattered on the floor, then turned for a table where I might put the cups down.

Lord Ruthven stood at my elbow.

My previous impressions of him were increased ten times over. Tall, slender, with a clear-cut profile, the only word coming to my mind was—Byronic. Like the great poet, he seemed to display an other-worldly appearance linked to reserves of strength. Not a muscle moved, yet one sensed power beneath the stillness: when required, he could strike with the speed of a pouncing cat. His face was quite without expression, but those penetrating eyes seemed to read what one was thinking.

In my present position, balancing a cup and saucer in either hand, he must have known at what a disadvantage I was feeling. The twins might have been struck into the likeness of marble statues, but I felt a fiery blush spreading from my neck to my forehead.

I bowed, shortly. He responded.

"Ruthven," he said.

"Aubrey, s-sir," I stammered. Feeling something more might be required, I gabbled, "Do you know Miss Wynter? That is—Miss Wynter *and*—er—Miss Wynter."

Two silent bows from him. Two silent curtsies from them. Then more silence. Indeed, how could one chatter about the weather to such a person as Ruthven? His celebrated pallor with its suggestion of death was violently contradicted by the life burning in those dark gray eyes. Still in black, unusual at afternoon tea, he made me feel like a clown in my blue jacket and yellow vest.

He smiled briefly. There was a concerted gasp from the twins. They had seen Ruthven smile!

"We must become better acquainted, Aubrey," he said. And left.

THREE
Found Dead

The day after tea with Lady Wynter I appeared in one place where I was sure there would be no chance of meeting Lord Ruthven: a coroner's court. My appearance there had been caused by the visiting card I left with the doctor. I was summoned to appear as a witness.

Witnesses and onlookers were crowded together in the whitewashed upper room of a pub—large enough for a party of drinkers but cramped for a court.

The coroner, a parchment-faced gnome, rapped on a scarred table in front of him, calling for silence in a room already as hushed as a tomb.

The testimony of most witnesses was of a dreary sameness. Drawn by desperate screams we had arrived more or less together and had found—what we had found.

The girl's father gave evidence with dry eyes, keeping calm by pretending that none of this was really happening.

"Yes, sir. I'm a men's clothing merchant. With my own shop. Yes, sir. She was our only child."

"Any known enemies?" Presumably, the coroner always asked this, whoever the dead person may have been.

"Enemies, sir? How would a fifteen-year-old child make enemies?"

"Kindly lower your voice," the coroner instructed

him sharply. Then he told him to stand down and called for the girl's mother.

"Your daughter left home to visit her aunt on the next street, did she not?"

"We hadn't thought she needed anybody with her just as far as the next street." The mother gave her evidence in a flat voice.

"But the body was found in a different neighborhood altogether, was it not?"

"We can't account for that, sir. Not at all. She'd never have gone off willingly with a stranger, sir. Not at all. I realize you're only doing your duty, sir, just as everyone here is doing theirs, but I want you all to know our Harriet was a good girl. As pure as a lamb. And whoever done this wicked thing . . ."

The coroner cut her short. "It is for the jury to decide whether, in fact, any wicked deed has been done," he said.

The testimony of two doctors—one of whom was the pompous person to whom I had handed my card—coincided.

"Death was not the result of an act of violence," said the first. "The girl's heart stopped beating, that is all."

The coroner asked, "Might it be possible to frighten a person to death?"

"Possible, but improbable."

The other doctor added, "I wonder if the deceased might have been suffering from some fatal disease. There was something about her blood—or lack of it . . ."

The father interrupted, shouting, "Our little girl was as healthy a child as . . ."

The coroner rebuked him.

15

The other doctor had also observed the deceased's throat. "There were two spots, like healed scars. Almost as though at some time recently she had been bitten."

"By only two teeth?" observed the coroner. "Do you know of any animals with only two teeth?"

"Only snakes," said the doctor, and admitted that this could not possibly have been a case of snakebite.

The jury was left to consider its verdict while the late afternoon sunlight slipped further and further down the window, until there seemed a likelihood of the court's being put to the expense of candles. Just in time, the members returned a verdict of "Found dead."

Those words seemed to break a spell, for the girl's mother gave a piercing shriek and crumpled, unconscious, into her husband's shaking arms.

The court was cleared.

As I emerged, shaking slightly myself, into the fading light, Ruthven stood opposite a pub door, as immobile and unconcerned as the sign on the door itself.

"My dear Aubrey," he murmured, "what quaint amusements you indulge in."

* * *

From then on our paths were constantly crossing.

For instance, there were forty or more young men gathered around the boxing ring in a field just beyond Chelsea.

"Rogers!" a hoarse voice was bawling. "I've a hundred pounds on you. There's twenty in it for you if you win."

The fight between Gentleman Rogers and the Welsh Basket had not yet gone more than twenty rounds. Very little blood had been drawn and the shouts of supporters were not sufficient to drown the thuds of bare fists on flesh. The boxers were evenly matched and looked ready to keep it up for another twenty rounds.

16

"Which of the brutes are you rooting for, dear Aubrey?" murmured a low voice behind me.

"Lord Ruthven!" Spinning round, I missed the Welshman losing a tooth to a straight right from Rogers. "I had no idea you were interested in boxing."

"My interests are wide," he replied. "For instance, how much do you stand to win on this match?"

"I've ten pounds on the Welsh boy, sir. And likely to lose it," I added regretfully. "I expected better of him. Now he's down."

Ruthven continued, "You've studied the subject?"

"I've taken lessons in boxing," I laughed. "Not to mention elocution, deportment, dancing, riding, fencing and shooting. No expense has been spared to turn a studious country lad into a young gentleman fit for the company of other young gentlemen."

"Successfully, it would seem."

"Thank you. But I needed every lesson. Six months ago I arrived in Town with a bank check, the address of a good tailor, and permission to make the most of my opportunities. You see, my guardian took a long time to realize that I was no longer playing with children's toys."

"Your—guardian?"

"My parents were both killed in a coach accident when I was ten. Oooh!"

My cry at that moment was caused, not by the pain of an old memory, but by a left hook which caught the Welshman on the nose. The onlookers were now served with as much blood as they could wish for.

"My dear Aubrey," said Ruthven softly, yet so clearly that I heard him above the shouting, "to become an orphan at an early age need not be counted an unmixed disaster. You are at least a free man."

I reminded him that I still had a guardian to whom I was accountable and a sister for whom I felt responsible.

"A sister? I have not heard you mention a sister before."

"I assure you, sir, I think of her all the time. Only, in these last months, there has been so much else to think about, too. . . . Oh, hit him, man!" I suddenly shouted, at last losing patience with the fight I was half-watching. "Hit him!"

"No need to become over-agitated, Aubrey. Your man will win."

"You're not even looking at my man." In my excitement I forgot all I had ever been taught of the rules of politeness. "Your eyes are always on the other."

"Quite so. Nevertheless your ten pounds are safe."

So they were. Rogers seemed to lose all his advantage from that point on. In the thirtieth round one blow from the Welshman knocked the wind out of him, while the followup stretched him on his back. He did not even try to get up after the count.

"My man won," I gasped. "You were right, sir."

"I usually am."

"How could you have been so sure?"

"That, my dear boy, is my secret."

He may have learned a lot about me, I thought, but everything about him was secret.

Rogers, just beginning to stir, protested that he hadn't known what hit him. Everything had seemed to go black.

We jeering spectators agreed. We had watched it happen.

I collected my ten pounds, then returned to the spot where I had left Lord Ruthven.

But Ruthven had gone.

FOUR
Money or Your Life

Lady Loveborough was giving a musical evening. There was an Irish singer from the Opera who had sung for Mozart, accompanied by a lady at the piano whose aunt had heard Mozart play. After refreshments there was to be a harpist and a flutist who were devoted to the memory of Mozart.

We sat on rows of gilded chairs in the Brook Street salon. Next to me sat Miss Jane Loveborough, giving all her attention to the trills and arpeggios while they were being played, and to me when they were not. I did not resent this at all as Miss Loveborough had a heartshaped face, brown intelligent eyes and a sense of humor. At least she laughed at my jokes, almost making me feel that I was as clever as I hoped to be.

She asked me if I knew what had become of Lord Ruthven.

"I saw him in the audience earlier," I said. "Then, at some point in the concert, almost in the time it takes to turn a page of music, there was a rustle and he was no longer there. He seems to come and go like that."

When refreshments were served, I escorted her to the adjoining room, then went in search of a fruit cup and some ices.

I returned with them to find her talking animatedly to a sturdy young man with hair like unraveled rope.

"No need to look so upset, Aubrey," she said, smiling.

"This is my cousin, Max. I think you should become acquainted."

I took to young Loveborough at once, if only because, by comparison, I passed as well dressed. His chest and shoulders seemed too broad to fit into his evening suit, and that hair defied any efforts to keep it flat.

Straight from school, he had been in town no longer than I had.

"I say, Aubrey," he said, "we might meet later this evening. My apartment is at the other end of Oxford Street. Just acquired a rather good red wine. Be grateful for your opinion about it."

"With pleasure," I agreed.

"There'll be a few other young men with high spirits, you know. A new deck of cards, and we'll have a livelier evening than we'd have at this concert!"

Miss Loveborough tapped his arm with her fan.

"Ah, yes," he went on, "won't do for us to leave the party all at the same time, though. Better slip away one by one. Then the old battleaxe won't notice. Oh! Beg your pardon, Jane."

"To which battleaxe do you refer?" asked Miss Loveborough. "Papa or mama?"

In my opinion, which I was careful not to voice, both Sir George and Lady Loveborough had what is called a commanding presence—though Lady Loveborough had the added advantage of a moustache. At this moment she was commanding our return to our chairs in the gilded music room.

Out of loyalty to Miss Loveborough (and perhaps to her heartshaped face and laughing brown eyes) I stayed to the very end of the concert.

By that time it was after ten o'clock and the street swam in silver light. The moon is a great temptress and I gave way to temptation. Having no carriage of my own, I should have hired a taxi; but the night was so fine that I decided to walk. After all, how far was it to the other end of Oxford Street?

I could at least have called for someone to accompany me, but where was the need with that great moon above?

I had not noticed the clouds.

The first part of my walk was cheerful enough as I strode along, whistling and swinging my cane. With an inflated opinion of my knowledge of the area, I decided to take a short cut. One side street was really as good as another.

The time came when I was not *quite* so sure of myself—only certain that sooner or later I must come to the main thoroughfare. Shortly afterwards, a massive cloud slid over the moon. Suddenly, every light in the world seemed to have been put out.

I had two choices—I could go forward or I could stay where I was until the moon came out again.

I imagined what a fool I would seem, clinging to the walls. Ah, the walls! As long as I could keep in touch with them, I would be guided. Tapping with my cane, I proceeded—not quite so merrily, but confident enough.

I cannot say exactly when I came to realize that there was someone else in the street, and not so far away at that. I cannot even say whether it was the sound of labored breathing or of shuffling feet that alerted me. I paused. The shuffling feet paused too, although the heavy breathing went on.

I prayed silently for the moon to shine again.

Then came the laugh. Low and diabolical. I had heard it before—on the night when the clothing dealer's daughter had been "found dead."

As the hellish chuckle was repeated, I gave up all

restraint and began to run. I could not see where I was running, knowing only that I had to move with all possible speed.

Something struck me forcefully in the chest, momentarily knocking the breath out of my body. It was the wall on the opposite side of the street.

For a few seconds I leaned against it, gasping, then turned around and ran again. My foot slipped on the cobblestones and I went down on one knee. At that moment, light flooded the street again.

A few yards away stood a giant scarecrow of a man, made even more evil-looking by his enormous shadow, cast by the moon behind him. The rags of uniform he wore could have survived every campaign from the Peninsula to Waterloo. In his right hand he grasped a knobbed club.

"Well," he breathed, slapping the club against a leather thigh boot. "Look wot we got 'ere. A prime pigeon. Turn out your pockets, my bantam, an' maybe I won't splash your silly brains all over the street."

Slowly I rose to my feet. I still held my cane, but realized that against his weapon it would be of less use than a hazel twig. Observing the way he began to raise his club in readiness and to convince him that I was a harmless milksop, I dropped my stick.

"That's the way, my young pal," he jeered. "Now hand over the money."

Could I trust him not to reward my offering with a bludgeon on my head? No, I could not. Nor was I inclined to turn and run again—those massive legs would soon have brought him up to me anyway.

Paradoxically, it seemed to me the only way of avoiding that massive lump of wood was to place myself too close for him to use it.

Smiling a stupid grin I leaped forward, almost knocking him off balance. Unfortunately not quite, but I did manage to enfold him in my grip, pinning his arms down by his side.

He tried to shake me off, like a large dog dislodging an annoying terrier. He was strong. I had not wasted my time at the gymnasium though, and I was desperate.

Closer now, I liked what I saw even less. With its bulbous nose, reddened by the elements and covered with scars, his face had the appearance of having been boiled too long. Although he showed a full set of teeth, they were black and broken.

He spat in my face. Instinctively I jerked away. Then he was free, with club raised.

A voice, low but penetrating, said, "Don't do that."

Any villain who knew his job would have brained me first, then settled the intruder. Perhaps this one, in spite of his bulk, lacked experience. He paused in mid-swing, just long enough for me to leap out of his reach.

Ruthven stood in the middle of the street, black and white in the moonlight, resembling even more a supernatural being. "You will put down that club." Not an order but an observation. "I say you will drop it."

The weapon fell to the ground.

Astonishingly the cutthroat began to whine. "I fought under Wellington at Waterloo. Bin fightin' for nigh on twenty year. Now the war's over, wot's an old soldier to live on?"

Imperturbably, Ruthven tossed a coin to the wretch. It gleamed in the air and rang on the ground. The old soldier fell to his knees, picked it up and bit it.

"A new one," he wheezed. "I'll drink your 'ealth, sir."He scrabbled after others as Ruthven threw more.

"Thank ye, sir. Oh, thank ye. Thank ye again. If only

23

I'd known the lad wos a friend . . . I swear I never meant to touch an 'air of 'is 'ead."

He scrambled to his feet, bowing and cringing as he backed away.

"You are forgetting something," remarked Ruthven. "That."

"That?" Bewildered, the ruffian glanced from Ruthven to the club, then back to Ruthven again.

"Take it," said Ruthven. "After all, it is the tool of your trade."

The wretch grabbed the weapon and hurried away, babbling incoherently.

I protested indignantly. "That object is deadly. He was quite prepared to murder me with it. Now he can kill anyone."

"Indeed," said Ruthven. "One day that club will bring him to the gallows. You and I will see him hanged yet."

"But four gold sovereigns too! . . . He'll drink it all."

"Naturally."

"Why?"

"Because he is already halfway to hell and that money will speed him on his way. Don't forget your cane or your hat. You appear to have discarded both."

As I picked up my belongings from the road, I thought, "I have not thanked Ruthven for his almost miraculous intervention."

He waved my bumbling gratitude aside.

"No miracle. When I had done—what had to be done—I returned to Brook Street only to learn that you had left a few minutes earlier. I spied you ahead and caught up with you."

With a shudder I recalled that evil laugh. "Did you see—or hear—anything else?"

"Only your robber friend."

"However did you manage to catch up without my noticing you?"

"I did not want our desperado to notice me, either. Even a moonlit night is full of shadows, and shadows are there to be used."

He accompanied me in silence as far as Max Loveborough's apartment, then refused to come up.

"Young men play young men's games," he said. "One day I may show you how one plays for higher stakes. One day. But not here. Not now."

We parted: I to wine and cards; Ruthven to who knows what. I drank and played, but not enough to leave me with a buzzing head or an empty pocket. When I parted from my fellow card players, gray dawn was just breaking and the events of the previous evening were already somewhat hazy.

I was reminded of them later that day.

FIVE
Grand Tour

With spring blossoming the mothers seemed to be laying siege in earnest.

Ruthven commented on my situation as we were trotting sedately through the park. "My dear Aubrey, an attack by a drunken brute is less dangerous for you than one by a soberly determined mama. While their husbands are hunting foxes in the suburbs, they are hunting down prospective husbands in town. Moreover, with the season's end in sight the chase grows fiercer."

I raised my hat as Lady Loveborough's carriage passed. Lady Loveborough bowed like a Roman emperor acknowledging the salute of a gladiator and, at a nudge from mama, Miss Loveborough, who had been watching children at play on the other side of the carriage, gave me a winning smile.

"The crocodile is also said to smile in greeting," remarked Ruthven. "Its subsequent tears are equally false."

"Miss Loveborough is a charming young person of both sense and sensibility," I protested. "In her own way she makes much better company than the Wynter girls—though I admit I feel safer with the twins. I cannot possibly be called upon to make an offer for both, so count myself protected from either. If only Amelia did not put on those languishing airs, or Arabella were not so inclined to play . . ."

"Play?" Could Ruthven's expressionless face have

become even stonier? "What a schoolboy may call a game, a sharp-eyed mama may consider a compromising situation—from which there would be only one honorable way out. I refer, of course, to suicide rather than the altar."

"I assure you, Ruthven, on this bright and sunny morning nothing is further from my mind than a glass of port wine and a pistol."

"Then, my dear Aubrey, I advise you to flee the country. With a young man as good-looking, as rich— as open, frank and unsuspecting—as yourself, the odds will not be on whether you will be caught, but on who will add you to her collection."

Some way ahead, a small commotion was taking place, but we could inquire about that when we reached it.

"Besides," Ruthven added, "I myself will soon be traveling abroad again."

My impulse to rein in my horse was checked only by the realization that I should then be expected to exchange pleasantries with Miss Wedman. "Leave England?" I blurted.

"I begin to pine for a harsher climate and wilder places."

The notion of Ruthven pining struck me as absurd— like the poet, Byron, with his reputed diet of vinegar and potatoes. Indifferent to everything, how could he want for anything? Inevitably, those dark eyes read my thoughts.

"What do you know of Ruthven?" he asked. "You have seen me only in England. Beyond its confines I am—quite a different being. Aubrey, I wish you would come with me."

What had Arabella said? "That voice could persuade

anybody to do anything." With all my heart I wanted to accompany him—who of my age would not have welcomed a chance to travel in such company?—yet I was also aware that, whatever the circumstances, I could not have refused. I felt that, out of respect to my independence, I must show at least token resistance.

"I—I am not entirely my own master," I stammered.

"Of course your guardian must be consulted."

"Until I am of age, he controls the purse strings."

"He is responsible for your education. Put it to him that if he should wish you to take the Grand Tour, I shall be delighted to act as your guide and mentor."

"Would you, Ruthven?" All reservations gone.

"My dear Aubrey, such an arrangement would be as much in my interest as in yours. But all must be settled quickly."

The Wynter twins and their mother in their carriage greeted me with a warmth they usually kept for near relations.

"For your sake as much as mine," said Ruthven.

The Wynter carriage was soon halted by the commotion near the park gate. Our horses paused alongside.

"How provoking," pouted Amelia, tossing her dark curls to show them to the best advantage.

"Not at all," cooed Lady Wynter, smiling sweetly in my direction. "We are in no hurry this morning."

"Indeed not," laughed Arabella, fair curls bouncing to outdo her sister.

"What appears to be wrong?" asked Lady Wynter.

I promised to find out.

Among the huddle of onlookers a stiffly-corseted, elderly, man looked up in answer to my inquiry.

"A girl, sir," he said, pleased to seem important. "Thought she was dozing in the sunshine. On closer examination—dead! No one can say how long she may have been there. Or what she died of."

On my return to the carriage I softened this morbid news as far as I was able.

"You need not have troubled yourself," remarked Ruthven, as the twins drove away with many backward glances. "If all the Horsemen of the Apocalypse were to ride by, the Wynters would merely ask if they were married or not."

As soon as possible I called upon my guardian.

He was a creaky old bachelor, living in a creaky old house which had been newly built immediately after the Great Fire, and was now over a hundred and fifty years old. For him it was conveniently near to the city with its bankers and brokers.

It was a rambling old building. Half the rooms were shut up and some he may never have seen inside. I had not entered the place myself more than half a dozen times in my whole life, the majority of those visits taking place during the last six months. His servants were few because his needs were simple. He was occupied with making money, not in spending it.

I believed money was food and drink to him—that he breakfasted on bonds and dined on stocks, with a morsel of a mortgage for luncheon. Not that he was miserly. He never denied himself anything he wanted—only all he ever wanted was to watch money grow.

In that respect the wisest thing my father ever did was to make a will ensuring that the financial affairs of my sister and myself were in this man's hands. Whatever might have become of our minds or our morals, at least our fortune was safe.

He could not understand why any young man should

want to make the Grand Tour. He walked up and down his dark-paneled study, sniffling and tutting.

"Tut-tut. Bless my soul." Sniff. "The Grand Tour you say?" Sniff. "The Grand Tour? Tut-tut-tut. What is this Grand Tour?"

As I knew that he knew perfectly well, I let him answer himself.

"Young men traveling abroad, expensively and uncomfortably, to pick up bad habits they could acquire more cheaply and agreeably at home." Baffled, he scratched at his wig, rust-colored and old-fashioned enough to sport a pigtail. Receiving no satisfaction from this, he removed the wig and rubbed his bald head.

"And what if I don't give permission, eh? You'll just take yourself off without it."

I protested that I should never do anything without his consent. To put his mind further at rest I emphasized that I should be under the personal protection of Lord Ruthven.

"Lord Ruthven? Who is this Lord Ruthven?"

As this was a subject on which I had little more information than he did, I held forth for awhile on the length of the line of Ruthvens, going back to the Dark Ages.

"Yes, yes, yes, my boy. That's all very well. But what about this one?" He kneaded a wrinkled, liver-spotted forehead with a wrinkled liver-spotted hand. "I've known of some drunks with dignified titles—sinking fast in a sea of debt and nothing but the title to bail out with. Remember Lord Ferrers, now. Hanged with a silken rope, they say. What do you actually know about Lord Ruthven?"

My account was brief.

My guardian resumed his rusty wig, sat behind his desk and tried to intimidate me by putting on a pair of steel spectacles. In the afternoon light, softened by dust, I could see there was a world of difference between my guardian's worthy black coat, from which no amount of brushing would remove the powdering of old documents, and Ruthven's black, which had the mysterious sheen of a midnight sky. I waited for my guardian to resume.

"So," he said, drumming his fingers on the desk top. "He has a persuasive voice and looks like Lord Byron. And on these recommendations you propose to trust yourself to this person as far as Rome?"

I replied, I hope not too boldly, that I should be prepared to trust myself with Lord Ruthven as far as China.

"Bless my soul! So far?" murmured my guardian. "It can't be done, y'know. There's no—what-you-may-call-it. No collateral. No security."

I insisted that there was nothing known *against* Ruthven.

That struck my guardian as a doubtful guarantee. In the case of default, who might be called upon to answer for him?

I suggested that, if my guardian were so concerned, he might make investigations. After all, with his city connections, he was better equipped than I for such research. If he were satisfied, surely there could be no further obstacles.

"Capital!" he crowed, and removed his steel spectacles. "The boy has a head on him after all. Put off the journey till we have unimpeachable references, then go with my blessing—for all the good that may do."

His face fell again when I tried to correct his mistake. That was not exactly what I had intended. Postponement was impossible, because Ruthven was sailing for the Continent in days rather than weeks. I added to the sense of urgency by hinting heavily at possible romantic entanglements I might do well to leave behind, quoting Ruthven on the subject.

This put the old gentleman in a quandary, wishing neither to keep me in the country against my best interests, nor to let me out of it in the company of a man lacking credentials.

I proposed a compromise—that I should be allowed to go, but that he should continue his investigation. He could write to me with his findings and I promised faithfully to act upon them.

He smiled again and rang for a bottle of port. It was the best—he did not deny himself anything he wanted. We drank toasts until he proposed one to my sister.

"To Lucy."

I was smitten by a sudden pang of remorse. Lucy! I must see her again—if only to bid her goodbye. She was younger than I and I had always felt responsible for her. In the years immediately after we had been orphaned we had been very close. After all, we had only each other. Yet in the past few months she had been seldom in my thoughts. In all that time had I been concerned with nothing but my own pleasure? My new life had indeed been rich and strange to me, but was that any excuse?

Our guardian, mellowed by the wine and the happy outcome of our meeting, beamed expansively. "Remember me kindly to her," he said. "Why, she must be quite the little lady. Thirteen or fourteen now, eh?"

"Seventeen," I reminded him. "At Miss Frobisher's Academy. Being finished."

"Ah, yes. Of course. Near Cheltenham."

"Near Bath, sir."

"Quite so. Another glass?"

SIX
Goodbyes

Miss Frobisher considered even the glimpse of a young gentleman likely to inflame sinful ideas among young ladies. Not possessing Ruthven's golden voice, I was compelled to use diplomacy and a frontal assault in order to say goodbye to Lucy.

After a tedious journey into Somerset I believe I might still not have seen her if my hired carriage at the door had not presented the Principal of the Academy with a *fait accompli.*

Miss Frobisher's brother, an elderly clergyman who taught geography and divinity, also put in a word on my behalf.

This allowed me time to convince the vigilant "watchdog" that my interest in Lucy was purely as a brother and that, as I was about to embark for foreign parts, our farewell must be now or never. Only then were the rules relaxed to allow us a few moments alone together.

As an extra concession—or perhaps for greater security—our interview took place in Miss Frobisher's own sitting room, profusely decorated with examples of her pupils' accomplishments. I had never seen so much needlework, embroidery and artwork crammed into such a limited space.

Lucy was as unlike either of the Wynter twins as could be imagined. Always a serious person, not only had

I never heard her giggle, but even a smile from her was a rare reward. She smiled now as she came into the room, her eyes lighting up like bluebells in the sun.

"Aubrey! Is it really you? Dear, dear Aubrey." She hugged me, rubbing her cheek affectionately against my scarf; thus no doubt confirming the worst fears of the Frobisher.

"Five minutes only, Mr. Aubrey," the turbaned watchdog snapped.

My sister recovered her composure and sat down sedately as though demonstrating an exercise in deportment. In this respect, though, the Academy had nothing to teach her. It was the way I always remembered my solemn Lucy.

Presumably satisfied, the watchdog retired, the door clicking gently behind her. I wondered whether her principles allowed her to listen behind it.

Lucy waited patiently for me to speak first. Somewhere a faltering duet was being practiced between an untuned harp and some squeaking instrument. Occasionally the piece bore a passing resemblance to Mozart.

"Are you—happy here, Lucy?" I asked.

"Oh, yes." By the way her face brightened I could tell this was the truth. "I have made so many friends. When we leave here—when we are presented in society—we shall still be friends."

"Lucy, as soon as I return, you shall be presented. That is a promise."

"As soon as you—return?"

"Oh, didn't I tell you?"

"You write so seldom, dear."

"I know!" I hit myself on the head. "I'm a selfish brute."

35

"Oh, I didn't wish to reproach you. You must be so terribly busy, learning how to be a man of the world."

I jumped to my feet, narrowly avoiding an encounter with a shell-framed water color on the table near my elbow.

"That is why I—came—here today." I had rehearsed this speech all the way from town, but still could not find a way to make it sound sincere. "It is terribly important for a man to be independent, you know. For that reason it is a good idea to—to leave everything that is familiar behind and to—to stand on one's own feet. That is why I am going abroad."

"Abroad?"

"To the Low Countries, to Switzerland, to Italy, perhaps even to Greece."

"Abroad!"

In the other room, practice ended with a resounding discord.

"Only for a year. Then you will be eighteen. You will attend your first London reception. I shall be with you again, and we shall be seen everywhere together." If only I dared to walk up and down. "Dear Lucy, don't tell me that you disapprove."

"No, my dear. It would be foolishly selfish of me to say that I wish you were not going. But when I think of the dangers . . ."

"Pooh! What dangers? The war was over long ago. Napoleon will stay on St. Helena forever, so there is no danger of that monster coming back to haunt us."

"There are monsters besides Napoleon," she said thoughtfully.

"Only in books."

"There are bandits."

"Who is afraid of bandits? I have learned how to use a pistol. At Manton's shooting gallery I hit the target five times out of six. Not exactly the bulls-eye, but at least I can hit the target."

"Avalanches, shipwrecks . . ."

"Nonsense. I tell you there is more danger on the streets of London . . ." I shuddered. Someone walking over my grave? I had a sudden mental picture of a doll-like face. Dead. I took Lucy's hand. "I—I am glad you are to be here while I am away. Promise me you will never go out alone until I return and go out with you."

Lucy laughed aloud at this absurdity and I forced myself to join in. Then we were both serious again.

"You must be careful, my dear," she said.

"Not only careful. I shall write to you regularly to let you know that I am safe and well."

"When I imagine you all alone in the middle of the Alps . . ."

"But I shall not be alone. I shall be with a friend. Lord Ruthven."

"A real lord?"

"How can anything go wrong when I am traveling with him? A lord will be better than a passport anywhere."

"Lord—?"

"Ruthven."

"Ruthven," she repeated. "I must remember that."

"Remember me," I said.

"Remember thee? Aye, thou poor ghost."

We laughed again. Years ago we had read *Hamlet* together, not understanding much, but enjoying the ghost and the murders. Now, though, in that small room, our laughter fell as hollowly as any ghostly voices.

37

"Like Hamlet's father, I shall come back," I insisted. "I shall come back again and again. You shall never be rid of me."

At that point Miss Frobisher came back, turban erect, her watchdog's jowls wobbling and teeth bared in the parody of a smile. I made my farewells. Under that ferocious glare I did not dare take Lucy's hand again or even murmur one more affectionate word. Instead I promised to describe every place of interest and to make sketches all the way.

In the feverish round of activities absorbing my time throughout the next few days, therefore, almost my first call was at a shop for artist's materials. I bought paper and pencils and crayons and watercolors as extravagantly as though I were setting up a studio.

"My dear Aubrey, we are about to visit the country of some of the world's greatest artists," commented Ruthven dryly. "Do you suppose such gear will be unobtainable there?"

With Lucy's loving face still fresh in my memory I bought everything just the same.

Ruthven approved my choice of pistols, though. According to one who knew the world, our English gunsmiths were the finest. He assumed that, if the occasion demanded, I would not hesitate to use my purchases.

During this time Ruthven was constantly at my side. I valued his advice, though his presence rather cast a shadow over my more tender farewells.

No doubt he knew what he was doing because, at my blunt announcement, the Wynter girls' giggles dissolved into wails.

Without Ruthven's intervention, my crude attempts at consolation might even have been interpreted as "an understanding." Under his cold stare neither was able to squeeze out one further tear.

Lady Wynter declared herself utterly confused at my lightning decision and—what was worse—my taking Lord Ruthven with me.

For, throughout every one of these interviews, Ruthven implied that I had been the one to suggest the tour and that he was merely following my wishes. Nor could I find the words to correct this impression.

Only when the final arrangements had been made did Ruthven leave me to my own devices. Then he would disappear for a day at a time.

When I tried to quiz him on his last-minute business, he would either turn the question against myself or not reply at all. Once, seemingly speaking while thinking of other matters, he did remark that he had been settling debts.

"Never leave a debt unsettled. Debts can leave a trail like drops of blood before a pack of hounds. A debt must always be paid. Always. Always."

SEVEN
Last Night

Our passage had been booked for the Channel crossing —Dover to Ostend. We were to travel from London to Dover with our baggage in a hired carriage. As this was ordered for six o'clock in the morning, I had a choice between wasting away the time with such pals as Max Loveborough or retiring to bed early.

Picturing my condition for a journey after carousing with a group of friends, I chose to spend the evening alone. But I had become totally unaccustomed to my own company. After an hour of gazing at a pile of luggage, and being by no means ready for sleep, I asked myself what Ruthven might be doing at this moment.

Might he also be at a loss? With so many future hours to be spent together, could he object to one more now? Although we had exchanged cards, he had never visited my lodgings, nor I his.

I took a taxi to the address on his card. At worst, he might not be in—in which case I was prepared to take another taxi back.

At first, I feared my effort had indeed been wasted. With full moonlight reflected from all the windows, no sign of life appeared within the house. Then I realized that the point of light in a window on the ground floor was a candle. So Ruthven might be at home after all. I rang the bell.

I received no answer. I waited, then rang a second

time, with the same result. Unwilling to give up so easily, I knocked on the brass lion knocker. At that, the door swung open a few inches, having obviously been left ajar.

I pushed at it and stepped inside. As I had come so far there seemed no reason not to go further.

The door of a room to my right being half open, I glanced inside. The bright light of the moon on the walls revealed patches where pictures had been taken down. There was no mirror over the mantle, no fixtures for candles, not even a chandelier—merely a hook in the center of the ceiling from which it should have hung.

A forsaken apartment if ever I saw one, without even a carpet on the floor. The only furniture was a wooden box by the window on which stood the candle I had seen, now burned down and flickering close to the socket of its metal candlestick.

Romantic notions from boyhood stories danced through my brain. Had that candle been lighting the room or had it been set there as a signal—or warning? To lure or to keep away?

Clearly Ruthven had nothing to do with it. In any case I assumed he would live on the upper floor. So I left the door wide open and began to mount the stairs.

Moonlight has a quality of dazzling brilliance where it is shining, which only intensifies the darkness of shadows. With doubts about venturing into unknown gloom, I went back for the candle.

I stumbled my way up the stairs and along a murky passage until I came to the door of the room at the front of the house. I tapped at it. Silence. I tapped again. Still silence. I began to have every sort of misgiving. Had some mishap befallen Ruthven? Was I in the right house? Was I dreaming? I groped for the door handle and turned it.

Though not as bare as the room below, this one had also been stripped of every semblance of comfort. By the window stood two plain chairs against a plain table. The floors, too, were bare. At least the chandelier was in its place. Was this Ruthven's apartment or was it not?

I could invent several explanations. With tomorrow's early departure, Ruthven could be spending the night at a hotel. He might even have been spending the last few days there, this house being cleared after he left.

In no way, though, could I account for the candle in my hand, burning for no one. As though aware that it had done all it had been intended to do, it sputtered out with a final spark and a twist of smoke.

I felt uncomfortable, but not afraid—until I heard footsteps coming up the stairs.

I called, "Is that you, Ruthven?"

The footsteps halted, then went down again. The front door shut with a heavy thud. I was alone in the house again, or so I hoped. I did not propose to remain much longer.

This adventure had given me enough to occupy my mind during the hours remaining until morning— always assuming that I might sleep without nightmares.

The expired candle was no loss because moonlight filled the room. I took a deep breath or so, set the useless candlestick on the table, then fumbled my way along the passage to the stairs again. All was well until, at the darkest point, I heard a faint sound, which stopped me with one foot outstretched for the next step.

I remained in that position until I had convinced myself that such a creak might be expected in any abandoned house. It may have been caused by no more than a draft under a door. I tiptoed down a few more steps. Until the laugh.

That same laugh I had heard twice before was enough to stop any heart beating. I was aware of my own still functioning by its thumping, which by rights should have been heard from cellar to attic.

I do not know how long I stood, only to realize eventually that if I held my breath much longer I would lose my senses. At last, admitting that I could not delay moving until daylight, I clattered boldly down the rest of the stairs.

The ground floor door was wide open as I had left it, the stark room still bathed in silver light. But a change had taken place. The wooden box had been moved to the center of the room. And from the hook in the ceiling, by a rope round his neck, swung the body of a man.

Perhaps I should have continued to run. A grisly fascination, though, drew me to this apparition. I could hardly convince myself that it was not a product of my imagination. I put out my hand to touch his foot and a dangling, buckled shoe fell off with a thud onto the bare floor.

As I stepped back with a smothered cry, a voice behind me remarked, "I do believe he is dead."

"Ruthven?" Immediately, I was jabbering questions and suggestions in a mishmash of incoherent gibberish.

"The explanation, my dear Aubrey, is simple enough. This man has hanged himself."

"We should inform someone."

"As you wish. You are aware of the procedures. A police officer is called; a doctor pronounces life to be extinct; witnesses are sought; a coroner's court is convened; eventually, a verdict is reached that the man hanged himself, which we know already. All this may take several weeks. Our carriage is ordered for six o'clock tomorrow morning. Do you want our trip to be postponed indefinitely—as it will be?"

"We can't leave him like that!"

"What else can we do? Don't concern yourself on his account. I assure you, *he* is past caring—least of all about who will cut him down. You can do nothing because you were never here." Then, as I still seemed to hesitate, a firm, "Come."

At the door Ruthven reflected, "At least that is one way to settle a debt."

I did not sleep at all that night and was ill all the way to Ostend.

EIGHT
Letters

Letter to Miss Aubrey, Miss Frobisher's Academy, Bath.

"My dearest Lucy,

Once again I beg your forgiveness for the tardiness of this communication. In fact we have barely paused in one place long enough for me to put pen to paper. We have passed almost at the gallop through Utrecht, Delft (where the pottery comes from), Antwerp (where there is a cathedral) and tomorrow our carriage must leave Brussels.

You will recall such tales of Brussels as the Duchess of Richmond's ball on the eve of Waterloo when the dancers whirled even as the guns began to boom. Or are such stories forbidden to young ladies? No matter, they will become all the more polished when I tell them on my return. Society in Brussels is every bit as sparkling as it must have been then.

I have been to the Opera where, in my opinion, the spectacle of the boxes with their fair occupants bedecked in silks and diamonds outshone anything on the stage. I have been to fashionable restaurants and to—so many other places.

I regret not having made sketches worth sending but have no wish to expose myself to the ridicule of your talented fellow pupils.

However, my ability is improving, together with my knowledge of languages. I can make myself understood, at least when demanding such necessities as cold wine and hot shaving water. I hope you continue well, as does his lordship and so indeed does your affectionate brother, Edwin."

Between Brussels and the Hartz mountains a letter from my guardian caught up with me. His neat, clerkly hand was better suited to books of account and such matters than to the affair now baffling him.

"Nothing has been discovered to the discredit of the person whom we discussed," he wrote, "although little else has been discovered either. The family under consideration is an old one and there is said to be a brother in the diplomatic service.

"I regret the delay in forwarding this scant information. Unfortunately, the employee entrusted to delve into these matters chose to hang himself on the evening before your departure from London. No one can guess why a man of previously sound mind should be so unhinged as to commit suicide in an empty house, with which he had no known association. Madness requires no motives.

"However, I write to put your mind at ease."

Put my mind at ease? He had brought back to it the memory of that body swinging from a hook in Ruthven's house.

A fire was burning in my hotel room. I threw the sheet of paper into the flames. It flared and was gone. If only I could be rid of my unease as simply.

As our tour progressed, my misgivings increased. Ruthven seemed infected by a fever for gambling. True, he would leave the tables hardly richer or poorer than when he sat down, but that only increased my worry. In spite of all I could do to dissuade myself, I was coming to believe that my friend could win or lose at will.

I wrote to Lucy as we passed through Switzerland, "You will see I find the mountains tolerably easy to sketch, particularly the confusion of rocks and wild torrents. I believe I can convey the awful chaos of a waterfall rather well. My pencil is not quite so sure when recording the more solid charm of an alpine chalet looking down over a valley of grazing cattle. Indeed, I have not attempted to draw a cow.

"I am enclosing only a few sketches because, after all, one mountain closely resembles other mountains, and one waterfall, even the most romantic, is very like another.

"Next week we cross into Italy. Soon we shall be in Rome.

"I expect Rome will be very different."

Different! Rome was different beyond all my imaginings. In the first place, the Roman sun outshone any other I had ever known. It flamed gloriously. Some may have complained of the heat, but to me it was life-restoring. Beneath its glow all morbid ideas evaporated. The effect on Ruthven was equally strong, for his gambling mania disappeared.

Under that sun, away went our strangulating ties (except when dressing for dinner, of course) and we now wore our shirts open at the throat. Yet, as it happened, we saw even less of each other. We were attracted to different Romes.

"I have business here," Ruthven said. That was all.

Some of his business must have been with a contessa. Not long after we arrived in the city, he took me with him to her palazzo.

With its great flight of stairs, high painted ceilings, statues and pictures, her palace seemed too grand for anyone to live in.

In spite of the growing heat of the day outside, the chamber where the contessa held court was cool. A striking young woman, she reclined on a couch in true Roman fashion, regarding us with half-closed eyes. I felt that she and Ruthven had much in common. Like Ruthven she favored black, but her simple gown had, in fact, been carefully chosen to show off the gems that adorned it.

Wearily, she stretched out her hand, heavy with rings.

After kissing it I looked up into her face and realized with a slight shock that she was not young at all. There were many fine lines on her forehead and at the corners of her eyes.

She asked why I was in Rome.

"I hope to improve my sketching," I said.

"So—an artist? In Rome you will find there are many beautiful models."

I quickly insisted, "My chief interest lies in ruins."

"We have many ruins in Rome, too." She smiled as though enjoying a private joke, and exchanged glances with Ruthven. "Do you know there are dungeons beneath this palazzo? You must visit us again, Signor Aubrey. Who knows, next time I may open my dungeons especially for you."

She held out her hand and I kissed it again before bowing myself out.

"Don't forget. You are to come again," she ordered.

For the first few days Ruthven and I had stayed at a hotel, then we moved into separate apartments in different parts of the city. Mine had a balcony overlooking a courtyard in which an orange tree grew, and in my bedroom was a brightly painted ceiling with clouds on which angels played musical instruments. The artist had been better than I was, but not much. Encouraged by his example, I took my sketchbook and pencils among the ruins.

After one of these expeditions I returned to find a packet of letters from England waiting for me. The first I opened was from Lucy. She had little news; what news could she have in her enclosed world? But she was still happy and still loved me. She hoped I was happy too.

The last letter was from my guardian. Written in haste, it was almost incoherent with hints, innuendos and naming-no-names. I had to read it twice before I could be sure what he was talking about.

Even then I could hardly grasp the message.

Something terrible had been discovered . . . Details could not be committed to paper: an agitated blot had to serve for that part of the story.

"There is no doubt that the person involved is vicious, capable of exerting an influence so evil that . . ." In turning the page my guardian had obviously forgotten how that sentence began and started another. "There have been innocent young women—for only the innocent could serve that monster's vile practices—bereaved families . . ."

Here the pen had spluttered so much that only a few words in whole lines were readable; but words that turned the afternoon heat into an icy chill. "Unspeakable habits," "danger to society," "unnatural powers of persuasion."

The worst of the letter was its vagueness. I was left to guess what may or may not have been done, and to whom.

The closing paragraph returned to my guardian's

former pedantic style, as though with an effort he had pulled himself together.

"You must leave your companion at once, and never see him again. You can decide for yourself whether to come home at once or to travel further. Whatever you do, put as much distance as possible between yourself and that—"

The apt word not springing immediately to mind, my guardian ended abruptly with "Yours respectfully."

In utter bewilderment I threw myself on to my bed and stared at the confusion of angels and clouds above me which seemed to reflect the confusion in my own mind.

NINE
The Italian Girl

Questions whirled around inside my head.

"How can I break with Ruthven? How can I accuse him of 'vile practices' when I have no idea what they might have been?"

Recollections of my schoolboy readings—midnight rites, unholy orgies, supernatural happenings—were prompting me to think the unthinkable.

True, he seemed to have some mysterious power of persuasion, but that is no crime. I could not even swear he used this strange talent at the cardtables.

I thought, "How can I believe young girls were involved when the evidence of my own eyes shows him to be quite indifferent to them?"

All this time I stared at the crude painting on the ceiling above me. Once so pleased with it, I could now only note how badly the artist compared with the worst on the contessa's walls.

The contessa! Why not? At the center of every scandal and intrigue in Rome, if anything were to be known about Ruthven's activities, she would know it.

I acted at once. Even in the heat of the afternoon.

When I sent in my card at her palazzo the contessa sent word through one of her servants that she was "at home" to me. With occasional sideways and meaningful glances, the man led me to an inner room.

It was much smaller than the one on my last visit, with a few carefully chosen paintings on the walls. Even in my agitated state I could not help noticing that they were all of a kind—Daphne pursued by Apollo, Proserpine carried away by Pluto, a Christian in the arena being savaged by a lion, all executed in meticulous detail.

"So you kept your promise, Signor Aubrey." The contessa waved me to a chair. "Have you come to see me or my dungeons?"

She ordered lemon drinks. While we sipped them I tried, as casually as possible, to steer our conversation from myself and toward Ruthven. After a while I realized that she, always smiling, could see through my blundering attempts to be diplomatic and was playing with me.

"Ruthven, Ruthven! Why are you asking always about Lord Ruthven and never about me?" The lines on her face were plainer to see now. She really was an old woman. "I have heard there is a girl who interests him. A sweet girl of a good family. Lord Ruthven is in need of young blood. But what of you! Shall we find a sweet young girl for you, too?"

I replied stiffly, "That will not be necessary."

She laughed aloud.

I tried to probe further, but the contessa was not prepared to reveal all her secrets at one meeting. A secret can be a valuable commodity, exchangeable for favors. She took pity on my anxiety just enough to reveal that the girl's father was a rich and worthy man—though perhaps too honest to survive long in the world of shadowy politics in which he was now involved.

"Oh, my dear, must you leave so soon?" she sighed. "Of course. You now wish to call on his lordship to find out if what I told you is true. It is, and he will admit it, because Lord Ruthven always tells the truth. Not always

the *whole* truth: but who can know the whole truth—
even about themselves.

"*Arrivederci.* Come again when there is more that I can
do for you."

In my state of mind that afternoon, the hand that I
kissed on parting seemed to me like a witch's claw.

I lost no time in getting to Ruthven's apartment. In
his shirtsleeves he was sitting at a desk, finishing a letter.

I did not interrupt and, while I waited, I glanced
around. Though plainly furnished, with white, undeco-
rated walls, this room was far less stark than that bleak
house I had visited in London.

I thought I detected around the place signs of prepara-
tion for a journey. I asked Ruthven if this was true.

"For a few days," he admitted. "I doubt if you will
miss me."

"Are you traveling alone?" I demanded, in my wor-
ried state no doubt far too bluntly.

His face was expressionless, but his dark eyes were
piercing. "Why do you ask?"

"Is—is there—a girl involved?" I continued.

He blotted and folded down the letter. After melting
wax at a candle by his side, he applied his signet ring to
the seal. Then he said, "Yes."

"I was told the girl comes from a good family."

"Yes."

"Is her family aware of this—this project?"

"No."

"What are you proposing to do with this girl?"

"That I cannot tell you."

"But she will be traveling with you?"

"Yes."

"For heaven's sake, are you intending to marry her?"

For a moment I thought he was about to laugh—and no one had ever heard Ruthven laugh. But he checked himself and merely smiled. "No."

"Are you aware of what will become of the girl if she runs away with you and there is no marriage?"

"Surely that is her concern."

"Mine, too. That girl could be my sister."

"Was your father a much-traveled man?"

"This is no occasion for joking. You know well enough what I mean. If I suspected a man of such intentions towards Lucy . . ."

"You would do everything in your power to protect her. That is only to be expected of a romantic young hero."

"I cannot stand by while that girl's life is ruined."

"But how will you set about this rescue? I know! You will inform her parents. But do you know their name or where they live? What a pity. Ah! This letter is addressed to her father. Why do not you take it to him personally? You will save the time of my servant, who is busy packing, and you can tell the signor all that you know."

"You are tempting me, Ruthven," I snapped.

"I am testing you, dear Aubrey. Do you really intend to stop me?"

"I shall do my best to prevent this elopement."

"Do what you will, it will take place tonight."

"Not if I can help it." I snatched up the letter before he could change his mind, but he made no move to prevent me.

"Aubrey, you are taking a great risk," he said.

I did not look back as I left the room.

* * *

The address on the letter was a villa outside the city, and I had to hire a coach. The afternoon was already late when I arrived at a honey-colored building, somewhat larger than my father's house in England, surrounded by carefully tended gardens.

An elderly manservant showed me into a large room on the first floor. The furnishings were rich without being extravagant.

By the window a group in the late afternoon sunshine might almost have been posing for a picture. The father, a commanding figure with a neatly-trimmed graying beard, stood behind his wife. The mother, an amiably plump person with a rather blank expression was enthroned in a heavily carved chair. They seemed surprised and puzzled at this sudden appearance of a hot and anxious eighteen-year old Englishman.

The daughter, a serious-faced girl who reminded me of Lucy, except that her hair was raven black instead of corn gold, stood up as I entered. I was just in time to see her expression change from delighted anticipation to disappointment. I was not the Englishman she was expecting.

In the best Italian families an unmarried daughter, newly out of convent school, is kept as carefully from young men of my age as any of Miss Frobisher's pupils. After the slightest greeting required by politeness, the girl was whisked from the room by her mother.

I am sure it was only due to the letter I brought from Ruthven that I was admitted at all.

Reading this, the signore seemed more bewildered. "Lord Ruthven send his regrets that he will be unable to dine with us tonight. You have put yourself to much trouble for so slight a message."

"That is Lord Ruthven's message, signore—not mine."

"And what is your message?"

"You—you may not find it easy to believe me, signor."

"I shall be better able to judge if you tell me."

"When—when Lord Ruthven leaves Rome tonight, he intends to take your daughter with him."

For a minute or more the signore was as still as a statue. Suddenly he hit the back of the carved chair with his clenched fist. "Young as you are, for such a slur on the good name of his daughter another father would ask that you name your weapons for a duel. I will at least give you the chance to justify yourself. How did you come by this information."

"From one I have every reason to believe."

The signore hit the chair again. "Who?"

"Lord Ruthven himself."

Silence stretched out. I saw the signore's jaw muscle twitch even under his beard, and wondered how well my fencing and shooting lessons would serve if I should be forced into a duel.

"Believe me, signore, I hope that I may have been mistaken," I said, when I could bear the tension no longer. "But, knowing what I know, I beg you to take precautions."

The signore took much more time to consider, then his daughter's personal maid was sent for.

As she came into the room, Annunciata, a severe, middle-aged woman, gave me a look part-questioning, part-fearful.

The dialogue between master and maid was conducted in a torrent of Italian so fast that I could not understand a word of it. From her gestures I understood Annunciata to progress from passionate denial to sulky agreement.

She turned to me. "You are so wrong," she hissed furiously. "I do as I am told, but you are telling one wicked lie."

Then she stormed from the room.

"Now she has her orders," said the signore. "Tonight she will not let my daughter out of her sight even for one minute. There will be no chance of any secret meeting —with his lordship or anyone else."

"You have put my mind at ease, signore," I said.

"I cannot say the same," he replied.

I had not made a good impression. I was not offered refreshment. I was not asked to stay.

I was not dismayed. I had other work to do.

That night I wrote to Ruthven, telling him exactly what I had done.

"After all that has happened," I wrote, "I will be leaving Rome as soon as possible. I think it would be better if we did not meet again."

While working on this farewell I found myself feeling unaccountably nervous, as though someone was looking over my shoulder. Although there was no wind, the balcony windows rattled as though someone was trying to get in. At last, irritated, I flung them open and was startled to see a dark figure looking up at me from the middle of the courtyard. Then I reassured myself that it was only the orange tree.

While tidying my papers I found my guardian's rambling warning. I burned it. It had served its purpose.

The next day Ruthven's servant brought a letter from him in reply to mine. He agreed completely to our parting. It ended, "Go, then. Remember my advice. Settle all accounts before you leave. As I always have and always will."

This too I put to the candle, but as I watched the paper blaze and blacken in the flame, I seemed to see Ruthven's dark, burning eyes.

TEN
Vampire

I left Rome the day after my break with Ruthven. I packed by throwing into bags and suitcases everything I needed, just as it came to hand. Anything that was not necessary for rapid travel, I gave to my servants. They were excited but not surprised—sudden flights were not so unusual, whether from angry lovers, outraged husbands or the secret police.

Before the night fell I was rattling away in a southbound coach, anxious to put many miles between myself and Ruthven as quickly as possible.

Night after night I saw in my dreams that expressionless face, heard those words "I always have and always will," and would wake up in a sweat, as though the message had some dreadful importance I could not work out.

From Naples I sailed from island to island, breathing the air of poets and artists. At the same time I improved my drawing and learned Greek.

Eventually, I came to my journey's end in Athens, city of glorious ruins.

At the edge of the city I found a room with a Greek family. My room looked out over a small yard with stables, but beyond were fields and woods and mountains. I thought that I would not be moving on for some time.

The couple who owned the house had one daughter —Ianthe.

Ianthe could hardly read or write. Her English was little better than my Greek, so instead of speaking she would often dance. Just as, instead of words, I drew lines on paper.

My skill with a pencil had improved. I could now sketch a pretty good likeness.

As Ianthe danced for me in a meadow near Athens I tried to picture her as a goddess. In the background, high on its hills, stood the Parthenon, white against vivid blue.

Eyes sparkling, Ianthe threw herself down beside me on the grass.

"Let me see picture. Let me see."

"It is not finished," I protested. "Perhaps it never will be. I am not satisfied with the dress. I want to copy more from statues."

"Please," she insisted. Then, delighted, "I look like that?"

"Much better than that," I assured her. "No mere drawing can compare with the living Ianthe."

She kissed me and jumped to her feet again. "We are now finished! Now we go home?"

I collected my materials, and we walked back to the city, she clinging to my arm, still half-dancing at my side.

What ridiculous creatures we men are—in our happiest moments we find fresh ways of making ourselves miserable! A new worry was beginning to trouble me. Now I was becoming too fond of Ianthe.

However, I did what any young man in my position would be expected to do. I pushed the problem to the back of my mind.

Day after day I explored Athens or its surroundings,

looking for antiques. Sometimes I even uncovered a fragment that had lain buried through the ages. Sometimes these expeditions on foot developed into day-long excursions further away.

Ianthe was always with me. I do not think she was aware of my growing feelings about her. As the days passed, though, I found these more and more difficult to deny to myself.

At last, to travel further, I bought a horse. This way, too, without hurting Ianthe by seeming to turn her away, I could spend whole days alone.

She always greeted me affectionately on my return. She would be waiting in the fields, straining her eyes in the direction from which I was expected. Finally she would run to meet me, arms outstretched, long, dark hair flying.

"Aubree. Aubree."

I would pick her up, set her on my horse and we would arrive home in style. This routine became so regular that I was sure the horse would perform it even if I were not on its back.

On my way back from one of these expeditions I rode into a village where a funeral was taking place.

I put on the expression of solemn reverence usual on such occasions, and reined in my horse to let the little procession with its flower-strewn coffin pass. The procession stopped too, with the coffin in front of me. Until this time all the villagers I had met had been warm and friendly. These, though, scowled and muttered. They made gestures to ward off the evil eye.

I had learned one trick on my travels. "When in doubt," I thought, "throw money."

This had no effect at all. Although as poor as most peasants, they let the coins lie in the dust. Some old women even spat upon them.

They grabbed white flowers that were lying on the coffin and threw them toward my face. Others tried to do the same, pressing against my horse so that I could neither ride on nor turn back. Although my horse was even-tempered and usually placid, there was always a chance that, if frightened, he might kick. . . . Someone could be hurt, and then my troubles really would begin.

A woman in the crowd began to point toward her neck. Others followed her example, shouting. This raised the excitement of the crowd to a fever pitch.

"I am sorry," I tried to explain in halting Greek. "I do not know your customs. I am sorry if I have offended you in any way."

This seemed to make them angrier.

"Stranger. Stranger," they shouted, and another word which I could not understand.

A younger peasant toward the edge of the crowd began to shout a different word.

"Brown." He pointed first to his own face and then to mine. "Brown. Brown."

The cries subsided to a grumbling and then died completely. Sullenly, those hemming me in moved away, partly shamefaced, partly annoyed at having been proved to be in the wrong.

I was free to go.

Before moving on I thanked the person who saved me.

"But why should the color of my face make such a difference?"

"Not pale," he said. "Not like death. In the coffin lies a young girl. She was murdered. She was killed by a pale man. Pale as death."

Vampire

This episode meant that the brief southern twilight was upon me before I reached Athens.

As I crossed the last field I saw Ianthe still waiting.

She was close to tears. "Why so long! Why stay until dark?"

Laughing, I told her my story of the angry villagers. Fearfully she repeated the word the villagers had shouted.

"Vampire."

"What does that mean? I have never heard the word before."

In her attempts to explain, Greek and English became hopelessly mixed. I must ask her father and mother. "They know all about vampires."

* * *

"I am surprised grown people believe such nonsense."

By lamplight, though, with the corners of the room lost in shadow, I felt a certain pleasant chill down my spine.

"You must have belief in vampires, Mr. Aubrey. You must," insisted Ianthe's mother. "If there is belief, there can be—precautions."

"Fairy stories!" I scoffed. "Have you ever seen one of these bloodsuckers?"

"Heaven forbid!"

"Then how do you know such fantastic creatures exist?"

"Do you believe in wolves, young man?" Ianthe's father slowly filled a pipe with strong tobacco.

"Of course I do."

"Have you ever seen a wolf?"

"No," I admitted reluctantly.

"Then how do you know such creatures as wolves exist?"

63

"Because I know people who have seen them."

"Ah!" Ianthe's father triumphantly pointed his pipe at me. "If you meet a person who has seen a vampire, then you will believe?"

"Only if that person has truly seen a vampire," I insisted. "Not just a person who knows a person who *may* have seen one of these things."

Ianthe's father and mother exchanged glances. What had I said?

"So. If we take you to her, you will come?"

"Only if you can promise that this person has seen a vampire with her own eyes."

"I will make all arrangements," said Ianthe's father. "The village is several hours' journey away."

"But I said . . ."

"This old woman has seen a vampire. You may not believe her, but you must hear what she says."

"Some day," I agreed, hoping they would soon forget. I really did not relish being made to look like a fool.

"The woman is frail,"urged Ianthe's mother. "She cannot live much longer. It must be soon or never."

"Soon," pleaded Ianthe.

"Very well," I agreed.

*   *   *

The old woman, wrinkled as a walnut, peered out through many layers of clothes. She had left her bed and dressed for this occasion. The villagers crowding into her tiny room treated her as a person of importance. After all, she had once seen a vampire. I, being a wealthy foreigner, was only second in importance, and given a seat of honor on a wooden chest.

Her story was told through looks, gestures and a rough translation into English by Ianthe's father.

"This Thing came from the north."

"From the mountains?"

"Not just a northern part of this country. Much further north."

"Transylvania?" I suggested.

"What does the country matter? The creature came to this village. It looked like a man and lived as one among us."

There was some nervous shuffling and sidelong glances.

"She was only a child when all this was happening," explained Ianthe's father. "This may have saved her life. The monster preferred girls of sixteen or seventeen. It fed upon their lives to prolong its own existence."

"How could it?"

"Their dead bodies were found, marked with the signs of the fiend's attack."

"What marks?"

"On the neck where it sucked their life-blood."

"All this happened many, many years ago," I said.

"The very old remember their childhood more clearly than they remember yesterday."

The old eyes were still bright, even though the old voice was cracked.

"The vampire was pale. Pale as death. With glossy black hair. Its handsome face was like one from a dream. Young women were easy prey."

More murmurs from the villagers. Few of the men there would be mistaken for a vampire.

"What happened then?"

The old woman shook her head.

"The Thing disappeared," translated Ianthe's father. "Perhaps men of the village killed it and buried the body where no one could find it. But she saw the Thing, the last one now alive who did. When she dies, no one will know what it looked like."

"No one . . ." The old woman's cracked voice dwindled to a mumble.

Ianthe, in a sudden burst of childish enthusiasm, told the villagers that I was a great artist and could draw a picture of the vampire for them.

I denied both these claims. "In the first place I am not as good as all that. In the second place I cannot make a likeness of something I have never seen."

"Now you hear the old woman's story, you can write it down?" argued Ianthe.

"Yes, but . . ."

"So why not the old woman tell what to draw?"

To please her I agreed to this comedy, and took out the sketchbook that went with me everywhere.

"Dark hair—so? Grecian profile—like this? Dark eyes in a pale face—there they are."

I drew as the old woman dictated. "Move this line up; move that line down; straighten this; curve that."

There was a great deal of crossing out and starting again. With growing unease and against all my instincts, out of that mass of scribble, smudges and erasures I made a fair copy.

When it was done, the old woman gave a great cry.

"She says that is the Thing. The Thing as it lived."

Everyone applauded as though I had performed some amazing trick.

But it was Ruthven's face on that paper.

Being a ceremonial sort of occasion, wine was brought out and gifts exchanged. I offered to leave the portrait with the old woman, but she did not want it.

"The picture will always be in her mind."

She waved it aside with a shriveled hand.

"Soon she will be dying and then it will only be something for others to fight over. But the little one, now . . . Once she was just so young and pretty . . . Such a pretty young thing should be able to defend herself."

After some commotion, a dagger was found in the chest on which I had been sitting. The hilt and sheath were elaborately decorated with identical designs. It was given to Ianthe.

Ianthe, delighted, kissed the old woman, then showed her present to me. Would I like to draw it?

I did not want to draw anything more that day.

ELEVEN
Death in the Woods

I should have destroyed the Ruthven/vampire picture at once. Unfortunately, I included it with all my other sketches of ruins, statues and Ianthe.

Ianthe seemed fascinated by the thing, as though trying to read a message in those penciled eyes.

One day, possessed by a demon of irritation, I snatched the drawing from her and, demanding to know what was so remarkable about such a piece of nonsense, tore it into four pieces.

At the shock of being treated so roughly by me for the first time since we met, Ianthe burst into tears. I had to comfort her.

To divert her I talked about the trip I intended to make next day. Recently, passing through one of the less accessible villages, I had picked up a rumor of an old tomb somewhere further north. By a mixture of guessing and calculation I had an idea where it might possibly be.

I drew a map for Ianthe of my intended route and illustrated it with tiny pictures. These were villages I would pass through; this was a stream I may have to wade through; this was the place where I might dig; these were the woods I might pass through . . .

"No!"

The laughter I had coaxed out of her was checked by a sudden cry of fear. "Those woods—no!"

"Why not? Woods are only woods."

"Nobody walk in those woods after dark. Not for any reason. Other creatures walk in those woods."

"What creatures? More childish superstitions."

She ran crying to her parents. They were equally horrified.

"Things not spoken of haunt those woods."

"Evil things."

"Bad things have been done there."

"We beg you to give up this idea."

"I am sorry, but . . ." I continued to be obstinate.

"Then at least come back a different way after dark."

"To do that I shall be forced to travel miles out of my way."

"Many more miles are better than taking such a terrible risk. If night should fall before you reach the awful place, you would do better to turn back and sleep on some peasant's floor, or even under the sky."

Their alarm was so real that I promised to do as they suggested. "I give my word to avoid the woods, going as well as coming back."

Gloom hung over the family next morning as I set out. Ianthe came to the side of my horse and begged me to be back before evening.

"If you are not," she declared, "I shall come out to look for you myself."

Those mythical beings apparently were at their most powerful after dark. She handed me a white, strong-smelling flower.

"Wear it for me."

"Could you not have found a flower that smelled somewhat sweeter?"

"This is garlic. The old woman say . . . here is the dagger she give."

"I have more powerful weapons in my saddlebag," I

reminded her. "English pistols are the finest in the world. Besides, I shall be happier knowing that you have the dagger with you. I am not afraid of vampires but of real villains. This country is notorious for its bandits."

"They are all in the mountains," she scoffed.

"There is no telling when others nearer may decide to take up the profession," I replied, solemnly handing back the dagger.

She, equally solemnly, swore to keep it by her always.

I took the long way around.

Those extra miles meant that I arrived at the place I was looking for much later than I intended. Even so, it seemed that my rough map had been wrong, for the day wore on with nothing but holes in the ground to show for my efforts.

I felt even more wilted than the garlic flower in my buttonhole. Angrily, I threw it away.

I was already more than half-inclined to blame everything on bad luck and return early to Athens, when a curiously marked stone attracted my attention.

Scraping away some of the encrusting soil I uncovered traces of carving. Annoyed by time already wasted, I worked furiously until the horned head of a satyr was revealed. The rest of him was still immovably underground, but my find had made all the laboring worthwhile.

"Ah, my uncouth friend," I thought. "Could it be your kind—half man and half goat—who haunt the forbidden woods?"

As if in reply came a mutter of thunder over the mountains. I looked up and was suddenly aware of the sun low on the horizon. If I did not hurry I would be caught by both darkness and the storm.

Though I was sorry to leave my discovery, there was nothing I could do. Now that I knew where he was I could come back tomorrow. In the meantime there was little chance of a stone satyr running away.

Although I urged on my horse, I knew I would be late. Night overtook me before I reached the outskirts of the forbidden woods.

For the briefest hesitation I was tempted to break my promise and take the quickest road—especially as, at that moment, the heavens opened. Even while I sat trying to make up my mind, I was soaked to the skin. But I had given my word. Though the longer way might be tedious, I could not become any wetter.

So I turned aside.

As it happened, the final decision was out of my hands. A bolt of blue forked lightning tore into a tree not fifty yards away. My horse screamed, reared and, in spite of all my pulling on the reins, plunged into the undergrowth among the trees.

Branches whipping at my face, I held on for my life, able to see only by the flashes of lightning from the storm that raged all around, spurring on my terrified mount.

A low-hanging branch, catching me in the chest, swept me from the saddle. As I hit the ground, a deeper blackness flooded over me.

When my senses returned, my horse was gone and the rain had stopped. There were still grumblings of thunder like some last defiant threats, preceded by occasional flashes of lightning. I was thankful for these, giving, as they did, the only light in my pitchblack surroundings.

Head still buzzing, I staggered forward. I was not certain where I was heading. I only trusted blindly that moving must be better than standing still.

By one of the last of those heaven-sent flashes I saw that I was near some hut. It was so small and tumble-down that its roof rose hardly any higher than the surrounding brushwood. It may have been uninviting, at least it offered shelter.

Then the screams began. I had heard screams like that before. I might have been standing again in a London street with a trembling boy at my side. There was no boy with a torch now. Nothing to guide me but a victim's soul-searing cries.

I smashed my way through the bushes . . .

I reached the hut, frantically clawing at the rough boards in my search for a way in. I found a latch but the door, if it was a door, would not budge.

I heaved at it with my shoulder until it burst open. At that moment, the dreadful screaming stopped.

There was utter silence in complete darkness, as though the world had come to an end and nothing existed any longer.

Then that detestable laugh. Low, evil, corrupt. I either had to scream with terror myself or to defy it.

I shouted, "Whoever you are, face me."

The reply was a pair of hands upon my throat. I had a choice—I could fight or I could die. I strove against a force that seemed more than human.

Briefly I managed to tear the hands away, but I was lifted bodily and hurled to the ground. Then there was a knee at my chest and the hands were squeezing away my life again.

Above the pounding in my ears I heard the sound of distant voices. Through the open door I glimpsed points of light. Suddenly the pressure was gone. Branches crashed as whatever it was broke through the woods. And I was alone.

Struggling to my hands and knees I crawled towards the approaching lights. Friendly hands helped me up. Friendly arms supported me. I recognized one or two faces in the torchlight.

"When the horse came back without you, the girl called us."

I tried to twist my lips into the semblance of a smile. "I understood—you Greeks would never walk in these woods—after dark."

"It was the girl. Called us cowards. Said she would come to you on her own."

"The girl!"

At my cry, the men almost carried me to the hut. The glare of their combined torches fell on the body of Ianthe.

Her face was waxen with no trace of color, not even around her lips. Her dress had been torn, exposing her neck. In her right hand she still grasped the ornamented dagger. Its sheath could not be found.

They say I screamed like a wounded animal. I do not know about that. I only know that I tumbled into an inky pool and the nightmares began.

There was the nightmare of hearing Ianthe calling for help and my being unable to reach her, blundering into obstacles and becoming lost in the dark as the cries died away.

There was the nightmare of seeing Ianthe, with staring eyes and bloodless lips, dancing with lifeless movements like a mechanical doll.

There was the nightmare of Ianthe joined by another doll-like face from another time, and by an Italian girl I had glimpsed only once; of the shadow of a man bent over them, pressing its mouth against each neck in turn; of my trying to shout a warning but being unable to

73

utter a sound; of them falling one by one—doll-face, Italian girl and, lastly, Ianthe. I struggled to reach that murdering shadow, but invisible hands held me back, held me down.

When I was helpless, the shadow turned to me. It was Ruthven, with blood on his smiling lips. Ruthven gliding toward me, whispering, "Accounts must always be settled." Ruthven, drawing closer and closer until there was nothing in my dream but Ruthven's face. And I found the voice to scream.

After that the delirium faded. The surrounding darkness was suffused with light. I became aware that what had gone before was hallucination and only this was real. Through half-open eyes I recognized the white walls of my room. A hazy figure was standing at the foot of my bed, looking down at me.

As I blinked and forced my eyes to open, the dark figure turned itself into Ruthven.

TWELVE
Death in the Mountains

I must have given a cry because he put a finger to his lips.

Was this still a fantasy? Sunlight fell upon the ikon of a saint, the only decoration on my wall. In the yard below a horse whinnied, its hooves clattering on the stones. They were real enough. So was this the worst nightmare of all—the one from which I should never be able to wake?

Ruthven spoke. "You will live," he said.

I struggled to raise myself, trying to ask twenty different questions at once.

"Rest," he ordered. "Now that I am satisfied you will recover I can leave you. I shall come again. In the meantime, you will rest. Close your eyes. The fever is past. You will sleep peacefully now. Rest."

I had no choice. Even without the influence of that persuasive voice, my weakness would have gotten the better of me. He was right. My sleep was now deep and calm. If I had any bad dreams, they were forgotten the instant I woke.

Of course, Ruthven came again. He was living in the same house, having persuaded Ianthe's parents to rent him a room. They told me that, during my illness, he had hardly left my side.

They gave fervent thanks for my recovery. At least they now had only one death to mourn. Ianthe had been buried days before, while I lay unconscious.

I blamed myself bitterly—if I had never mentioned those cursed woods, she would not have ventured into it.

They would have none of my self-accusations. Wherever she had gone, there could have been no protection against the vampire. My injuries showed how hard I had fought to save her.

On my throat were still two purple bruises where the beast's thumbs had pressed. I had barely escaped with my own life.

Much of my recovery I owed to Ruthven's nursing. He had known exactly what had to be done and there had been no going against his instructions.

"At least I prevented the doctors from bleeding you to death," he remarked, urging a cooling drink upon me. "I could not allow mere leeches to succeed after a more violent attempt on your life had failed. Besides, my dear Aubrey, in the time I had for reflection at your bedside, I came to the conclusion that I could ill afford to lose you. I need you, my boy."

"How did you appear so opportunely?" I wanted to know. "Your being in Athens was an amazing coincidence."

"No coincidence at all. I was looking for you. I had not expected to find you burning up with a fever. The soaking you received in the storm did more damage than your attacker."

"But why should you look for me? After our quarrel in Rome . . ."

"Quarrel? I remember no quarrel. I merely agreed to your request. You wished to travel alone. Who was I to prevent you?"

"That girl . . ."

"Forget the girl. I did." He smiled. "As for seeking

you out, I understood we were friends. Friendships must be kept in constant repair."

Throughout the following days I grew stronger. At least I was able to eat and drink, Ruthven masterfully ordering food that would hasten my recovery. At last I was able to walk a little.

Ruthven accompanied me as far as the seashore. Together we watched the surface of the water ruffled by the breeze.

"You must be bored," I remarked. "This is a poor substitute for gambling tables or parties."

He replied, "Have you known me so long yet so little? I care no more for a society ball than for a fish market. I have more to concern me than winning or losing—at cards or anything else."

He returned to his contemplation of the sea.

Throughout my convalescence, as during my fever, he was never far from me. He seldom left the house, except during our walks. On these, he must have noticed the effect they had on me.

It was impossible to move in any direction without being reminded of Ianthe. Every stone, every tree, every view had its associations. I even found myself starting to speak to her, then realizing she was not with me and never would be again. My body was recovering but my mind was not.

"You need a change of scene and air," Ruthven insisted. "You cannot be allowed to rot away. That is all very well for some things, but not for intelligent beings. Greece is all sea and mountains. Let us explore the northern regions together."

By this time I was so sunk in depression that I was completely indifferent as to where I might be. So I agreed.

Ianthe's parents were only slightly less annoyed by this proposal than they had been by my previous excursions. Everyone knew the mountains to be full of bandits, prepared to cut a traveler's throat for the clothes on his back, let alone the money in his pockets.

In my present mood I would not have greatly cared if a bandit's bullet had cut short my misery then and there. Besides, argument against Ruthven's wishes was not only a waste of breath, it was short-lived.

Ruthven hired men to accompany us.

"Better qualified to act as guides than as guards," he remarked, when the weatherworn group assembled for inspection.

"We know the mountain tracks as surely as any goat," protested their leader. "Enemies? We laugh at enemies."

"But will you fight them, too?" asked Ruthven.

"We do not believe such talk. Is put about by the mountain villagers to frighten travelers. So you are paying for protection. Such dangers are all in the mind."

Mountain villagers, when we met them, merely shrugged. We were crazy, but we were English, so that was only to be expected.

Between villages, I would have enjoyed the cliffs and forests. Instead I climbed Mount Olympus itself, with no greater thrill than I might have felt in climbing a ladder.

I can only say that with bracing air, plain food and constant exercise, my health improved.

The landscape became increasingly wild, with rough tracks over bare peaks suddenly plunging through deep gorges.

"If bandits exist at all," observed Ruthven, "This wilderness must be the place where we will find them. Or they us," he added.

We were following a mountain stream in which the water foamed against boulders that had crashed down from overhanging precipices. After a while the valley narrowed, until we were riding with a torrent on one side of us and a wall of rock on the other.

"If ever a trap were designed by nature, this is the one," said Ruthven.

When we were halfway down the pass, with no chance of escape, a bullet whistled past my ear. It had been a warning shot to advise us that resistance was not only useless but foolish. Our attackers had not planned on our being reckless fools.

We tumbled from our horses, and made for the cover of rocks, the guides firing back in the direction from which the first shot had come.

More by chance than calculation Ruthven and I found ourselves protected from the main onslaught by an outcrop of rock in a slight bend of the valley.

The first burst of wild firing did no harm, as the bandits wished to frighten rather than hurt, and our men were shooting at hidden targets. After a while the tumult died down and I noticed a colored scarf waving from a boulder near the top of the cliff.

A man shouted down to us in Greek. "Throw away your guns and we will treat you as guests. Continue to resist and we will kill you all."

One of our guides shouted a particularly offensive insult, to which the bandit replied by threatening to feed our livers to the eagles.

A burst of gunfire followed. Short, because neither side wished to waste bullets.

"If we are to be murdered by robbers, at least we are dressed for the part," reflected Ruthven.

By theatrical standards, in our embroidered jackets

and brightly-colored scarves, we looked more like bandits than our attackers.

Facing danger I felt fire in my blood again.

Although his expression was as inscrutable as ever, there was a gleam in Ruthven's eyes. "This is an interesting predicament," he commented. "We cannot stir without being exposed to their gunfire. Yet we cannot stay in this position indefinitely. We would die of boredom if of nothing else. What is more important, those ruffians have the freedom to move along the peaks and take us from the rear whenever they choose."

The entrenched parties were now calling to each other. "Unmanly cowards." "Unmentionable swine."

"That fellow up there, leading the shouting, seems to be their leader," observed Ruthven. "If he were out of the way the others might be persuaded to negotiate."

"Easy to say, but how can it be done?"

"No doubt he thinks himself secure enough in his rocky fort," said Ruthven. "But a sure shot from the far side of the stream might bring him down before he realizes the danger."

"I'll do it," I cried eagerly.

"Don't be a fool," remarked Ruthven, coolly. "It must be done with one shot or not at all. At the shooting gallery you learned to hit your target five times out of six, but how often did you score a bull'seye?"

"Are you so sure that you can do it?" I countered. "A dash across that flood will be as dangerous for you as for me."

"I never take unnecessary risks," returned Ruthven. "Now, I think. While they are still exchanging compliments."

Before I could reply, he was up to his thighs in the swirling stream, his gun held high to keep it dry.

He might have succeeded if one of our party had not at that moment loosed a shot at random. This brought a brief hail of bullets from the other side.

One caught Ruthven in the shoulder. He spun and fell.

At that moment I saw nothing but a companion in deep water. I ran from cover and plunged into the torrent. Buffeted by the swirling currents, I held him up and, part lifting, part dragging, brought him to the opposite bank. He lay unconscious, wet and bleeding.

When I looked up, I found myself surrounded, not only by our own guards, but by bandits. Ruthven's summing up of the situation had been correct—but in reverse. The moment our men saw Ruthven wounded, they immediately threw down their arms and surrendered.

I cursed them in every language of which I had an inkling. The force of my rage was such that Ruthven was lifted carefully by men of both sides and carried to a cave higher up the valley.

This was furnished with such small comforts as might have been expected in the circumstances—rough beds of branches covered by filthy blankets, a cooking pot and a fire.

This was the room set aside by the bandits for their temporary "guests." To the rear it led nowhere and the entrance could be guarded by a single gun.

Ruthven's wound was dressed with such crude ability as the rogues possessed.

Gathered around they were a sorry group, dressed in an assortment of looted garments from military tunics to dancing shoes. Even after his ordeal Ruthven appeared better dressed. I thought I caught one or two of the desperados eyeing his embroidered jacket, however spattered with mud and blood.

Their leader spoke for them. A middle-aged bearded man, shirtless from choice rather than necessity to impress onlookers with his muscular build, he had the swagger of an actor. Perhaps most of his life had been spent in giving such performances as this. Now he was all apologies.

"This injury was an accident. Quite unintended and bad for business. We have to keep our visitors alive and in good health. Who will pay ransom for a dead man?"

Ransom terms had to be negotiated before anything else was done. Much as I hated parting with a penny to these cutthroats, I had no choice. To myself I justified the payment as a penalty for my own foolishness in not listening to repeated warnings.

Ruthven lacking the use of his arm, I wrote the letter to Athens, requesting that the bearer should be allowed to return safely with the amount mentioned.

The messenger left with orders to make all possible speed. The bandits wanted the money in their hands and, almost as urgently, the wounded man *off* their hands.

This may have been the reason why they agreed so readily when I insisted that Ruthven be left in peace. Even the sentry took up his position some distance from the mouth of the cave.

Ruthven's eyelids fluttered. "How much did they demand?" he whispered.

Shamefacedly I told him what we were being forced to pay.

"How disappointing," he murmured. "I had no idea I was thought to be worth so little."

Then he drifted into sleep again.

Fever gripped him. At least, I assumed so from his thirst, from the way his lips cracked and burned, and from the way in which he lay without stirring. Yet his face was never flushed, always keeping its usual pallor. Indeed, at times, when his eyes were closed and he hardly seemed to breathe, I was afraid I might be watching over a corpse.

"Do not worry, dear Aubrey," he breathed, seeming to read my thoughts. "When that happens, you will have no doubt."

"Not when," I insisted. "Not even if."

"It is when for all men," he replied. "Mere mortals are born to die. All—men." He smiled faintly. "All—men."

After a few days I could see that his arm was worse. Even after repeated washing the infection had spread. I could smell the decay. Surgery might have saved him, but there were no surgeons in these mountains. On the evening of his last day he knew that he was dying.

I tried to deny it.

"My arm is dead already," he commented. "The rest of me will soon follow. There is very little time to do what has to be done."

He fixed his eyes intently upon me. The flame of the crude lamp by the bedside flickered on his face. The dancing shadows gave it the illusion of expression. I could not sit idly by and watch him slip away.

If only there was something I could do. Either my agitation showed in my expression or he guessed my thoughts.

"You can save me, dear boy," he whispered.

"Can I? How?" I cried. "Tell me."

"Oh, not my life," he continued. "I care as little about my passing as I do about the day passing. But, lying here, I have begun to fear for my reputation."

"Your reputation is quite secure," I insisted.

"Is it? Have you overlooked our parting scene in Rome?"

"That is past and forgotten."

"And what gave rise to it, too? Why did you begin to mistrust me? On what were your suspicions based?"

When I did not reply he went on, "No need to hang your head. All this is finished. But I would not want it to be remembered to my discredit."

I declared that, as far as I was concerned, those disagreements were over and done.

"That is not quite enough, dear Aubrey."

I wanted to know what more I could do. He had only to ask.

"I want you to swear."

"Swear?"

"Swear an oath that you will hold as sacred."

"Swear—what?"

"Swear that you will never report to a living soul anything that you know of me—or even suspect of me. Swear that you will never even speak of me. Not even to spread word of my death here."

"How can I—?" I began to protest.

His good hand seized my wrist tightly. I tried to draw back, but it was impossible. I had never known such strength in a grip. For an instant I thought this could not be a dying man. My fears must have been groundless.

He continued to pull me down toward him, his eyes fixed on mine. Our faces were so close that those burning eyes were all I was aware of. They seemed to fill my universe like two dark, smoldering pits. Beyond them his voice rose.

"You will not speak of me. You will be unable to speak of me. You will die rather than speak of me. Swear."

"I—I . . ."

"Swear!"

"I swear."

Slowly his grasp relaxed. His arm fell back. His eyes were no longer looking at me. They were no longer looking at anything. As always, he had been right. When it happened, I had no doubt. Ruthven was dead.

The damp walls of the cave glistened in the feeble light. When I stood up, my shadow merged with all the others. The place was dark and uncomfortable, but no longer mysterious. Some feeling of mystery had died with him. I closed his eyes and left the cave.

The bandit with the gun looked up. I wanted to tell him what had just happened, but felt too choked with emotion. So I merely gestured. He nodded, as though I were merely confirming something he had been expecting, and went in to where the body lay. No need to guard me. There was no risk of my running away.

The moon had not yet risen, so I had to fumble my way as I teetered down the mountain track. I wanted to think of all that I had just seen and heard.

As soon as the bandits were aware of Ruthven's death, there was sure to be hubbub and bustle. I needed to be alone.

The dark was profound on the valley floor. I sat down with my back to the nearest boulder, and tried to collect my thoughts. "What had Ruthven been trying to say?" I asked myself. "Why that over-dramatic charade of a solemn oath? And his eyes . . ." I did not want to think about those eyes.

As I sat, the moon rose. It was a full moon. The sight of it filled me with an unaccustomed serenity, quite at odds with the turmoil of my life over the past year. The night air was warm, and I was exhausted with watching over my patient. Sitting there, I fell asleep.

I was wakened by the early sun shining on my face. A rock for my pillow had been hardly less comfortable than the sleeping arrangements provided by my captors. Just as the blood returning to my stiff limbs brought on an attack of pins and needles, so the memory of last night erased any bright thoughts the new dawn might have brought.

Woodenly I climbed the path to the cave. Inside, all was chaos, with shouting, threats, accusations and counter-accusations. The body of Ruthven had disappeared.

The accepted belief of the majority was that one or more of them had buried it secretly after stealing the clothes. To their leader this constituted treachery, deceit, disobedience, and a threat to his authority. He was determined to get at the truth by the quickest possible means.

He roared for silence, which came almost instantaneously. He surveyed his men, face by face. He knew them all, maintaining his position as much by his ability to judge character as by the strength of his arm.

He knew when to use that, too. The guard of last night was lurking on the edge of the group, as though trying not to attract attention. Without a word the chief hit the man, who fell—also without a word.

The chief then turned to the unconscious guard's nearest companion. This unfortunate man, without waiting for a threatening word or gesture, fell to his knees, begging, if not for mercy, at least for a light sentence.

He was hauled to his feet and allowed a breathing space for his defense.

"No clothes are ever stole," he protested. "Nothing. We only did what we promised his lordship."

"I know nothing of this," I said.

The man agreed. "His lordship wait until you are away from the cave for a few minutes. Then he make demands. Demands they are though he say please. We cannot refuse. Besides, it seem such a small thing to ask. It couldn't do no harm."

"What was asked?"

"That when his lordship die, his body be take to a nearby rock. Is left to lie as he say 'under first cold ray of the moon that rise after my death.' That we do. The body is lying on the mountain top all night. If you ask the other man before you strike him, he tell you this story is true."

"There is another way to check this story," growled the chief. "We all go to the spot where you leave his lordship's body."

There was no body.

There was only a slab of rock on which a body could have laid.

There were uneasy mutterings among the brigands. Where had the body gone? How could it have gone? What could have taken it?

"Ah, but look!" Their chief swept a commanding hand over the rugged surroundings. "All around are ravines. A body can be tossed into any one of them after its clothes are stolen. I am not intending to search them all."

On his knees, the accused began to babble. "How can I be guilty of such a theft? Do I possess any such rich clothes? Search my belongings. Nobody will find among them any colored scarf or embroidered coat."

"A mind so crooked as to invent that story of moonlight magic would easily be able to find a clever hiding place," argued his leader.

The bandit's punishment was immediate and painful. I was beyond caring. Too much had happened too quickly. I was sure Ruthven would not have cared, either, where his abandoned body finally lay.

If he could have spoken he would have accepted this last indignity with a wry comment, just as he had mocked the demand for his ransom.

The money arrived a few days later, and I was freed. The leader of the bandits even set me on the right track. When we parted, he was still apologizing for the unfortunate accident that had resulted in my returning to Athens alone.

THIRTEEN
Damning Evidence

Once I had thought I could never tire of Greece. Now I longed to be back in England. The sooner I started, the sooner the voyage would be over.

I wrote to Lucy and to my guardian. The letter to my guardian was businesslike. I asked for funds to make up for unexpectedly large expenses. I did not mention ransom: he might have thought that I was incapable of looking after myself.

With Lucy I intended to be more honest. I felt the need to tell her of the events of these last weeks.

When faced with a sheet of paper, though, the ink dried on my pen, and I merely wrote, "I am coming home."

I began to pack.

I could not imagine what was to be done with Ruthven's few belongings. For some reason I could not bring myself even to mention them. Then I had the idea that somewhere among them might be a clue to his family or other friends.

His possessions were all as unrevealing as the man himself—until I opened one last traveling bag.

Among other small items I found a drawing which had been torn into four pieces. Fitted together these formed my portrait of a so-called vampire that might have been Ruthven.

My eyes were telling me something too horrible to be thought. The bag also contained the sheath to a dagger, ornamented in a way I recognized only too well. The same decoration was on the hilt of the dagger Ianthe had been grasping when she died. This was the missing sheath.

Ianthe's killer himself was now dead. "Lucky for you, Ruthven," I cried aloud. "Otherwise I should have killed you with my own hands."

The horror was not done yet, though. The Italian girl had been part of my fever-dream. Was that merely my sick imagination, or was she another victim of Ianthe's murderer? I could not rest until I found out.

I came to Greece by way of Italy. There was no reason why I should not return the same way.

* * *

I called again at the honey-colored villa just outside Rome.

I found it empty. The gardens, left untended for months, were already ragged and overgrown. I walked around the outside of the villa, peering in at windows, trying to find a clue as to what may have happened. Without success.

Should I call on the contessa again? She must surely know something. But what of those significant glances I had seen passing between her and Ruthven? Those two may have been unholy allies.

I was walking back to my carriage when a woman in black came hurrying towards me from the road.

"Signore, Signore," she called.

I recognized her as the maid, Annunciata.

"I see you arrive, signore. You have news, no?"

"I am sorry," I said. "I am myself seeking news. Do you know what has happened to this family?"

"Tragedy upon tragedy." Her words came in such a rush that I had difficulty in translating them for myself.

"Someone turn the master in for his political activities. One day he is took away. People who go away so do not come back. The mistress, poor soul, go out of her mind and is taken to a different place. The English lord do all this to us." She grasped her black dress as though she meant to tear it. "But I am to blame, too. I open the garden door to him. But he talk so soft and the young mistress beg me."

"The young mistress," I insisted. "What became of the young mistress?"

"Nobody know. She with his lordship the night before he leave Rome. She is not heard of since."

The woman broke down in tears, apologized for such foolishness in front of a stranger, and hurried away again.

My coach drove from the deserted villa as from a funeral.

I had left England many months before. The Grand Tour was to have put an experienced head on a young colt's shoulders. It had succeeded only too well. I would never again be the carefree young fellow I once was.

FOURTEEN
The Hanging

I held Lucy's hand as our carriage rolled sedately through the spring sunshine toward the entrance of our country home. I was bringing her from Miss Frobisher's Academy to Aubrey End.

Just as the year's first buds were unfolding, so I hoped a new life was about to begin for both of us.

As the carriage swept around the final curve of the drive, the great front door of our house opened. A boy appeared at our horses' heads. I waved aside the footman who materialized at my elbow and myself helped Lucy down from the coach. For some time to come, I would be taking care of her.

I had asked for the servants to be assembled in the entrance hall—from butler, housekeeper and cook to undermaid and gardener's boy—so that they might welcome my sister. The oldest of them had known her as a blue-eyed, reserved little girl. I wanted them to realize that, although still blue-eyed and reserved, this young woman was now mistress of the house.

She spoke to each in turn, greeting the old-established members of the staff by name and asking the names of the rather shy recent additions. After much bobbing and curtsying, they went about their duties.

Taking my overcoat and hat, the butler murmured, "Mr. Armitage is in the library, sir."

Our guardian put down the book he had been pretending to read and held out his hands.

"Upon my soul, you've changed. Both of you."

He had not. With the same dusty black coat, the same rust-colored wig, and the same way of reducing the world around him to columns of figures in a ledger, he was here because there were urgent matters of finance to talk over. It showed this growing regard for us that he had suffered the discomfort of a coach journey north instead of summoning us down to him. Perhaps he wanted to keep us away from the temptations of London until the final details of Lucy's future were settled.

"The last time I was in this house . . ." he began, then stopped himself. "Dear me. Melancholy occasion." Blowing his nose, he dismissed the memory. "But what's to be done with you now, eh? What's to be done with both of you?"

He knew as well as we did. The question was not "what?" but "how?" I had promised Lucy that London season so necessary to every young lady. Husbands do not drop from trees, but have to be sought out.

The current season was already half over. We might have chosen to wait another six or seven months, but that seemed hardly fair to Lucy. By next fall she would be nineteen, and there were at least three months of balls, receptions, teas and introductions ahead.

However, young ladies must be formally introduced to society by persons of quality.

"What is more," I argued, "they need a good address at which other young ladies may call. A London establishment."

"A London establishment? Tut-tut-tut. Of your own? Oh, no, no, no. That will never provide sufficient guarantee for Miss Lucy's reputation."

"But I shall be with her."

"A brother does not count as a chaperone. In any case

I do not consider the additional expense to be necessary." He clasped his wrinkled hands together as though afraid the money might be slipping through them.

"It is, after all, our own money, sir," I reminded him.

"After you reach the age of twenty-one you can spend your way into a debtor's prison as speedily as you choose. Until then I am responsible for balancing the books on your behalf."

He marched up and down the library, clearing his throat, tut-tutting and blowing his nose. I began to wonder why he had put himself to the expense of a journey when a simple "No" would have been enough.

"As for your apartment, young sir," with a slightly embarrassed sniff. "Why be put to the expense of renting an apartment when my house is big enough for two single men? You can be accommodated comfortably enough. Within reason, you can call upon the services of my domestic staff. Far from living in each other's pockets, there is no need for us ever to meet, except occasionally on the stairs."

"Sir," I remarked stiffly, "behind these suggestions lurks a suspicion that I am not entirely reliable in my choice of companions."

He waved a forgiving hand. "That is all behind us now and need not be mentioned again. True, the house is not in a fashionable district, but you are not expected to be at the center of fashion."

"But Lucy . . ." I began.

"Ah, Lucy . . ." He busied himself putting on his severe straight-sided spectacles, then looked through them anywhere but at us. "I have made–not inquiries, but investigations somewhat more delicate.

"Lady Loveborough holds you in high regard, my boy. You are acquainted with her nephew, are you not?"

"Indeed I am, sir."

I did not tell him that Lady Loveborough did not have in mind my friendship with Max so much as a more permanent attachment to her daughter, Jane.

"Lady Loveborough, it seems, will be delighted to have Lucy stay at her house in Brook Street. She has always regretted her Jane being an only child, with only a mother for companion. Two girls will be company for each other. Of course, you, young man, will probably also be in regular attendance."

At last our guardian brought himself to look us in the eye. "Those are my proposals. I consider them sound. You are not obliged to accept them."

We accepted.

Soon our house was shrouded again in dust sheets. In our absence, though, it would be well cared for and, at the slightest notice, would be ready to welcome us again.

We were made equally welcome by Sir George, Lady Loveborough and Miss Jane. With much of the season over, I suspect we made an agreeable change of faces. This was Jane Loveborough's second season, as it was for the Wynter girls. They were all very friendly toward Lucy—knowing that wherever she went, I would not be far behind.

Over tea, though, the Wynter twins openly criticized the effect of the Grand Tour on me.

"I'm sorry it has made him so dull," pouted Arabella, still tossing her curls in the way she considered provocative. "Have you not noticed the difference, dear Jane?"

Dear Jane, smiling, considered my dullness more attractive than many another man's brilliance.

"One would think that a person taking the Grand Tour would come back with something to talk about," sighed Amelia, with the limp wave of her hand which she had been practicing.

"Oh, Aubrey wrote to me regularly," said Lucy, rushing to defend me and then blushing at her boldness. "Anyone may read his letters if they wish."

"Who would wish to read letters that anyone may read?" said Max Loveborough. His aunt had insisted that he cancel a planned afternoon at Manton's shooting gallery in order to be at her tea. "No revelations."

"Indeed, Aubrey has not revealed one thing," Amelia went on. "He even started the tour with Lord Ruthven and came back without him. What was the reason for that? And where is Lord Ruthven now?"

I pretended not to hear, hastily asking Lady Loveborough her opinion on the relative merits of Vauxhall and Ranelagh Gardens.

"You see how annoying he can be," complained Arabella. "He becomes conveniently deaf at the first mention of a topic everyone wants to hear about."

"There are some topics I would rather not talk about," I said, rather primly.

The silly girls could be most provoking. How could I explain I was bound by a solemn promise? A promise is a promise—even when made to a murdering beast. Even when the beast is dead.

"Miss Wynter is right," drawled Max. "You have come back to us a boring dog, Aubrey. If that is what travel does to a man, I must be grateful to my family for keeping me at home."

"I'm sorry," I said. "I must have outgrown some of my old amusements."

"Then we'll have to find something new for you."

Suddenly he slapped his knee with the force of a pistol shot. "I say, of course. Why not come to the hanging?"

Lady Loveborough, startled at his outburst, splashed tea into her saucer. She repeated heavily, "A hanging?"

"Hanging," confirmed her nephew cheerfully. "Fellow being turned off—day after tomorrow. Half a dozen of us chipped in and paid for a window. We can squeeze together to make room for Aubrey. What do you say? I'll lay any odds you've never been to a hanging before."

"I am not sure that I want to witness one now," I replied.

"They say it beats cock fighting," said Max. Then he added thoughtfully, "Though there can't be any betting on the outcome." At this point he caught a freezing look from his aunt.

"Aubrey is right," said Jane Loveborough. "It cannot be a pleasant exhibition, no matter how much the criminal may have deserved his punishment."

"Deserve it?" cried Max. "Of course he deserves it. A fellow can't go knocking out a fellow's brains with a cursed great bludgeon and not expect to pay for it."

"A bludgeon?" I repeated. "He—killed a man with a bludgeon?"

"Stole his watch, too. Impudence! Caught trying to sell it. Jeweler recognized it from an advertisement. Set up a hue and cry. I suppose the murdering thief must have left his club at home. The big, drunken brute lived by highway robbery since he was discharged from the army."

After this information a silence fell over the drawing room. A tiny clock on the mantel whirred and chimed the hour.

"He must be counting the hours now," said Max.

"That is quite sufficient, Maximilian," said Lady Loveborough, with a massively commanding gesture.

"As Aubrey says, there are some topics we prefer not to talk about."

At the back of my mind I seemed to hear the echo of a distant voice at another time. It said, "That bludgeon will bring him to the gallows."

I knew that, after all, I must be at the hanging.

The window, hired by Max and his friends, was on the first floor of a gin shop facing Newgate Prison.

The owner, who made a regular income from the public executions which took place opposite his premises, was prepared for the party. Because of his experience with high-spirited young gentlemen, he had hidden all movables and breakables in rooms to the rear of his house, where the windows looked out on nothing more fascinating than a dismal yard.

The rented room contained half a dozen chairs, made to stand up to boisterous treatment, and a table with a top stained by the repeated spilling of beers, wines and spirits. This did not matter to us, as the mess was covered by a white tablecloth, prudently added to our picnic basket.

Starting out at five o'clock in the morning had sharpened our appetites. Disregarding the grim ceremony to follow in a very few hours, we breakfasted heartily on cold punch and game pie as though this was to be a day at the races and not the last of a fellow being's life.

Cards had been included among the provisions, and we played until we heard the clock of St. Sepulchre's church strike half past seven. Then, in case we would be missing anything, we took our places at the window.

This was opened wide, partly because of the grimy condition of the glass, and partly to allow those at the front of our party to lean out while those at the back leaned over them. Three of us at the front bunched together on chairs, while the others stood behind.

A scaffold jutted out from a little door in the prison wall. It consisted of a raised platform with a ladder against it. At one end were two black posts topped by a black crossbar. The gallows. Looking down slightly, I could just make out a trap door between the two posts.

A crowd of over a thousand was packed into Newgate Street. No doubt the thieves would be doing good business picking pockets—as long as they had sufficient room to ply their trade.

Very few of the faces below me seemed to be those of ruffians. Mostly they appeared sober, respectable family men. Some even had their families with them. At least one boy was riding on his father's shoulders for a better view.

As the clock struck eight, an expectant hush fell over the crowd. The door in the prison wall opened, and a small group of men mounted the ladder to the scaffold. First came a tall, grave man in black, next a burly brute with his hands tied in front of him. It was difficult to tell whether he was being supported or restrained by two officers. He was not meekly accepting what had been ordered for him.

He faced the crowd, shouting curses at them all. Even if I had not recognized the blotched and bloated face, the memory of that gravelly voice would have identified him. This was indeed the villain who had threatened me. Without Ruthven's intervention, my brains might have been those knocked out by the same murderous cudgel.

The criminal was forced to stand between the posts. The man in black pulled a white cotton nightcap right over the condemned man's head, stifling the stream of abuse. The entire street fell silent.

In the room behind me I heard the door open.

As the man in black slipped a noose over his victim's head, a voice behind me said, "That bludgeon will bring him to the gallows."

This time I knew that the voice, low and clear as I remembered it, was not in my head. Trying to twist in my seat to find out who had spoken, I was held by those behind me pressing forward. As my gaze left the hooded man, there came a gasp from a thousand throats like a monstrous expiring sigh—followed by a cheer.

When I looked back, the man on the scaffold had disappeared. All that was to be seen now was a taut, swaying rope. Like the pendulum of a stopping clock, it slowly came to rest.

A slight argument broke out as to the exact time this had taken and as to who owned the more accurate watch. The pressure around me eased.

Above the claims and counterclaims of who had counted how many seconds, the unforgettable voice continued, "Why so disturbed, dear Aubrey? Did I not say that we should see him hanged? And have we not seen a man hanging before, you and I?"

Although I had more freedom to move, Max pressing against the back of my chair meant that I could not stand up. He was arguing, not because he had just lost a wager, but because he liked arguments. In spite of all my struggles all I could see were the brass buttons on his plaid vest. I butted it with my head.

Max staggered back, bleating, "I say . . ."

I leaped to my feet, looking wildly around.

Our party, and only our party, occupied the room. The door was shut. I rushed to it and flung it open.

The narrow passage and stairs were now crammed with people emerging from other rooms on this floor and even from the attics above. The face I was looking for was not among them.

Why should it be? His body had been left in the Greek mountains. I had seen him die.

I closed the door and stood with my back against it. Around my neck my shirt collar felt clammy.

"I say," repeated Max. "You look terrible." He ruffled his string-colored hair in a gesture of puzzlement and concern. "Get him a brandy, somebody. The poor fellow's never seen a man hanging before."

The words were similar, but the voice was so different. It had not been Max who spoke earlier.

"Which one of you was—talking to me—while it was happening?" I demanded hoarsely. "Who mentioned the bludgeon?"

The others looked at each other with blank, uncomprehending faces. Not one of them had the imagination for such a trick. A chair was pushed up behind me, and a flask of brandy thrust into my hand.

"Drink up."

"Soon feel better."

"I say, should we stick his head between his knees?"

To convince them there was no need for such extreme measures, I took a deep breath and assumed a cheerfulness I did not feel. As far as I was able, I became one of them again.

"Really silly of me," I laughed. "I'd be obliged if you didn't mention it."

All jolly good fellows at heart, they understood perfectly. Not a word of my weakness would pass their lips. For my part I was determined that, in future, the only executions I would witness would be in a play—at the theater.

FIFTEEN
Remember Your Oath

The Theatre Royal, Drury Lane, was green and gold and crimson, lit by enormous crystal chandeliers.

Lucy absorbed the scene seriously enough, but her blue eyes were sparkling with excitement. We amused ourselves before the performance looking for faces we might recognize among the audience. There were nearly two thousand other playgoers, dressed for the occasion. The ladies were dazzling with their feathers and fans.

I took her hand. "Happy, dear one?" I asked.

"Oh, yes. I don't know when I have been so happy."

"Lady Loveborough advised me to take a box seat open to the rest of the audience," I said. "Private boxes give less chance to see, and almost no chance of being seen. For Lady Loveborough that is the sole purpose in going to the theater."

"Lady Loveborough believes I do not take enough pains to make people notice me," sighed Lucy. "She forgets that I have been in London no time at all. Let us both forget about being seen and enjoy what is happening on the stage."

For two hours Edmund Kean's Richard III held us with his smiling villainy. Only the ghosts toward the end of the play were a disappointment, making most unghostly entrances through trap doors. I smiled at Lucy and she smiled at me.

"Acceptable, perhaps, if one believes in ghosts," I whispered, "but comic when one does not."

"The man in the box opposite us looks more like a ghost than any on stage," she whispered back. "How pale he is. But how handsome. I think Lord Byron must look like that. Jane Loveborough described Byron to me. She has seen him. Could that be Lord Byron?"

"Lord Byron is out of the country," I said with a feeling of dread.

"How he stares in this direction. He seems to find you most interesting, Aubrey. He cannot take his eyes off you. But you are not looking at him."

I did not want to look. At last I had no choice.

At first I did not recognize his face. Perhaps I did not want to. He had a lean and hungry look. But there could be no mistaking those devilish eyes.

It was impossible! I had watched the man die. I had closed those glazing eyes. Yet there he sat. All other eyes were upon the stage, his dark eyes were unblinkingly upon me.

"I do not believe in ghosts," I told myself.

If I did not believe in ghosts, though, what was that thing in the box opposite?

"Do you know him?" asked Lucy.

"Shush. Watch the play."

Forcing myself to set an example, I tried to concentrate on the final scene, when Richard fights "as one drunk with wounds." I saw nothing of this, though, waiting only for the burst of applause that would allow me to turn my head again.

When it came, the figure in the box opposite us had gone. I jumped to my feet. This gesture was misinterpreted, for I started a standing ovation. Kean bowed in my direction.

"Are we to leave now?" asked Lucy. "Is there not a comedy to follow?"

"There is . . . We shall . . . Stay here. Refreshments —coffee—ices . . ." I muttered, leaving her blinking behind me as I made for the door of the box.

I had to make my way to the other side of the building. I had to know that my eyes deceived me.

Outside, the corridor was filling with others making their way to the bar and to the refreshment rooms. My view was obstructed by feathers, and by fashionable piled-up Grecian hair styles. I could not elbow my way too vigorously without the risk of treading on some lacy under-petticoat.

From the box corridor, down the great staircase, across the lobby, I hurried. How could one face be picked out of this mass? Unless it were also looking for me.

Up the other staircase and down the box corridor opposite. The doors were all open. I would wait here by the seat opposite in his box. Ghost or double? I intended to know.

I was between doors when my wrist was seized from behind. Without seeing him, without hearing him, I recognized that grasp like iron. I tried to turn. Useless. I was held helpless.

"Remember your oath!" rasped that hated voice.

"It *was* your voice!" I gasped. "At the hanging."

"Whose voice did you think it was?" it asked mockingly.

"I saw you die."

"Mere mortals are born to die."

"And dead men stay dead."

"Indeed *men* do."

"You couldn't . . ."

"There are more things in heaven and earth . . ."

104

"What are you?"

"Ah. That requires explanation. Impossible here. At another time, and in another place, dear Aubrey."

"Let me look at you, you devil."

"Meanwhile, you can be sure I shall never be far from you."

"What are you doing here?"

"Warning you, in case you may be tempted to break your word. Your sacred oath, remember. Let me remind you of it. You will never again speak of me."

I struggled to break his hold, infuriated by his calm assurance that I was still prepared to be a partner to his crimes.

"When I swore that oath I did not know what you were. I refuse to be bound by it."

"You will discover that you are bound." The voice near my ear was now so low that only I could have heard it. "Others are coming back from the bar. Your sister will be wondering what has become of you. How thoughtless of you to neglect her for so long. See."

He thrust me forward into the doorway. On the opposite side of the theater Lucy was looking to the right and left, fluttering her fan. She was not nervous, because she had such trust in me, but I was now aware of my foolishness in leaving her unprotected. I was also aware that there was no longer a grip on my arm.

I spun round. People were returning down the corridor towards their seats. He was not among them.

My return was slightly easier than my coming, because there was no longer the hurry to reach the refreshment rooms. I reached our box shortly before *Raising the Wind* was due to begin.

"There you are, my dear," said Lucy, smiling so that I would not think she was criticizing. "Did you not find the refreshments?"

"Too great a crowd," I replied, shortly.

As I sat down I put my hand on the rail in front of me. On my wrist a purple bruise was already beginning to show. Hastily I pulled my cuff over it.

Fortunately Lucy was still intent on the activity around her. "The man opposite us has not returned," she observed. "Perhaps he does not intend to remain for the comedy."

I did not tell her there was no need. For him most of the comedy had already been played. How many acts were still to come?

* * *

I had no doubt that we should meet again—when he wished. No longer supposing a bullet to have ended his power to do harm, now I knew the monster was still walking the streets of London, as strong and deadly as ever.

What could I do? Much as I longed to see a rope around his neck, I could not picture Ruthven on a scaffold. He would always think up some way of escaping ordinary justice.

I had stopped him over the Italian girl. At least I had delayed his scheme. If only I had stayed in Rome a little longer, I might have defeated him completely.

My guardian had been to blame for that. If only he had not insisted on my breaking with Ruthven immediately.

My guardian, of course! Among his reports on Ruthven he would have evidence. I had only to add mine and we would have proof enough to alert the authorities. . . .

I was invited downstairs to join my guardian by his fireside and share his evening wine. The first glass he drank in silence, contenting himself with observing, from time to time, the glowing coals on his old-fashioned hearth through the rich wine in his glass. After our second refilling, he said, "You wished to tell me something, my boy?"

Wished? I was bursting. I strained to speak. But, with growing desperation, I realized my mouth was refusing to frame the words my brain was ordering. I could not even hint by a nod or wink the horrible details raging in my mind. I sat blank-faced and speechless.

My guardian lifted his wig with one finger and scratched behind his ear, obviously becoming uneasy. What confidences might a young charge have difficulty in putting into words? He sniffed, hummed a line or two of an old song, then asked, "In the best of health, are you, my boy?"

I assured him that I was.

"Not quite as lively as usual, I fancy."

I supposed late nights sometimes had that effect.

"Nothing to do with money, is it? No plunging at the races?"

I put his mind at ease on that score.

"Well, then?"

"I—I—wished to give you my word that—that—all is well with me, sir," I blurted, and dashed from the room.

As I closed the door I heard him mutter, "Upon my soul."

Swearing that solemn oath in the cave had cast a spell on me. Now I recalled how, in writing home, I had been unable to form words on the page; how at the theater I had left Lucy believing I did not know the man. So that

107

was why Ruthven could feel so sure of me. I could never say anything that might harm him.

I tried once more with Max Loveborough. Once again I was struck dumb. Seeing me apparently gasping for air, Max became quite concerned.

"Upon my life, Aubrey, I do believe your condition is worse than before. Better provide some diversion."

My tongue was loosened again. I reminded him that his last outing to Newgate Prison had cast me into a state of depression that lasted a week. Did he now have the lunatics at Bedlam Insane Asylum in mind? He pooh-poohed this notion. What I needed now was a walk into Vauxhall Gardens.

I took him up on the idea at once. I should have thought of it myself. It would make a wonderful evening. I could escort Lucy and he could take his cousin—or the other way round, if he preferred.

He did not prefer either. I had in mind just you, me and a few other likely chaps to kick up our heels. Can't do that with one's relations on one's back. Besides, I doubt if my aunt would approve of Vauxhall. After all, anybody can walk in, just by paying."

* * *

In spite of his disapproving head-wagging, I put the suggestion to Lady Loveborough over my next dinner at Brook Street. She did not at first say "Yes," but she did not immediately say "No."

"Vauxhall is a place where young persons might find themselves in compromising situations," she remarked, as fish was being served. "Indeed, it has no doubt answered that purpose before now."

By dessert, though, she had softened. "I see no reason why a party would not be acceptable—as long as it is large enough. There is safety in numbers. For instance,

the Misses Wynter might be invited to join us, and
suitable escorts arranged. . . . Maximilian, please refrain
from rolling up your eyes in that absurd fashion I
understand the entertainment can be most pleasant.
Some quite respectable persons attend, even though they
may be in business."

"Vauxhall, you say?" At this point Sir George
Loveborough, at the head of the table, intervened. He
breathed heavily, as though eating his way through a full
dinner took as much effort as running a race. In his case
perhaps it did, for his usually red face always became
crimson as the meal progressed. "Ah. Vauxhall."

I assumed he was about to forbid the jaunt. On the
contrary, he was taken with the idea. Seeing how the
other classes enjoyed themselves might, for once, make
an agreeable change from cards at his clubs. He was
inclined to join the party himself.

From one point of view this was as good as canceling
it. The look on Max's face was plainly asking how a
fellow could possibly enjoy a night out when surrounded
by uncles, aunts and cousins.

SIXTEEN
After Dark at Vauxhall

With Lady Loveborough organizing, little was left to chance. We took two carriages. Sir George, Max, Lucy, Arabella and the Honorable Augustus Snoad occupied one; Lady Loveborough, myself, Jane and a Captain Beverley traveled in the other. Amelia Wynter had taken to her bed, red-eyed and sneezing, having denied until the very last moment that she was suffering from a spring cold. This made her Captain Beverley one annoying escort too many.

However, I am sure Miss Jane found Captain Beverley a far more entertaining companion than myself. In spite of the combined efforts of music, charming company and fairy lights, a heavy feeling of dread settled on me.

When we reached Vauxhall, thousands of lamps were already twinkling. At the heart of the gardens, among acres of ornamental trees and bushes, stood a gilded rotunda, around which pavilions and arbors were grouped.

Our party was established in a pavilion from which we could watch the passing crowd. Sir George ordered champagne for the men and cordials for the ladies.

Fiddlers in the rotunda struck up a lively tune, and Sir George, entering into the spirit of the occasion, asked, "Might there be fireworks later, my man?"

The waiter replied, "There might werry well be fireworks."

Some people are uneasy if a cat comes into the room.

In the same way, the hairs at the back of my neck prickled. I could not say what I feared, but I had a feeling of something dreadful quite near.

I was so preoccupied that I missed several remarks addressed to me by Sir George, thus giving the impression that I was either deaf or an oaf.

At last this feeling of apprehension grew so strong that I could no longer stay seated. As I jumped up I glanced down the path curving around our pavilion. By a clump of lilacs a few yards away, dark eyes fixed on me, stood Ruthven.

He beckoned.

At the next table Sir George paused in the middle of a story that seemed to have no beginning and showed no sign of ending.

"I say," laughed Max, "what does Aubrey find so fascinating?"

Confused, I began to apologize to Sir George.

"Ah, now we see," said Max, "Well worth looking at."

Below us strolled a well-to-do family—father, mother and daughter. The father and mother, well-rounded from years of good living, were in their Sunday best. The daughter, as Max had pointed out, was pretty in a blue flowered muslin gown. Her new bonnet was obviously intended to draw admiring and envious glances. Around her shoulders she wore a lacy shawl, which could have done little to keep off the evening air, but which served to attract attention to her slender white neck.

As she passed, the girl looked up at me, half-pert, half-innocent, pleased with herself at having made a small conquest.

Lady Loveborough inhaled a long, slow breath. Arabella giggled.

"I did not . . ." I stammered, blushing. "I—I was looking at—at . . ." I could not name what I had been looking at. I could not even lift my hand to point in that direction. Besides, there was no one now by the clump of lilacs.

That beckoning gesture had been a summons I could not ignore. Without looking where, I put down my wine glass. I could not even tell whether it found the table by chance or whether someone took it from my hand.

I mumbled a request to be excused, and stumbled down the pavilion steps, only just aware of the abruptly silenced chatter behind me. Fortunately this was covered by fiddlers in the rotunda pitching into a high-spirited dance.

I made my way through a maze of twisting and complicated paths, under the delicate lamps. Set among the greenery to add mystery rather than shed light, these were now doing their best to compete against the rising moon.

My search took me down dim alleys with rustic seats on which lovers were more closely intertwined than the vines above them, through tunnels of branches bent overhead, by grottos and arbors in which couples sharing bottles could feel themselves part of the fun yet apart from it.

In one of these arbors Ruthven stood, waiting.

"You knew I would be here tonight," I challenged him.

"My dear Aubrey, I know more about you than you can possibly comprehend. My destiny is bound up with yours."

"What do you want, you demon? Why are you here?"

"There is so much that you want to know," smiled

Ruthven. "You will not thank me for telling you, but you shall know."

"What are you? Where did you come from?" My voice rose to a shout.

Ruthven raised a hand to quiet me. "You think of yourself as being known as a man. I know only that I am a different kind of being."

"You are an abomination!" I cried. "Evil. Evil!"

"I do not even know what you mean by evil," he said evenly.

"You have killed and killed again. I know of three victims. How many more there may have been I dare not think."

"More than you or I can count," was the cool reply.

If only I could have struck him down at that moment! Without a weapon, I could only cry, "Why? Why?"

"You eat, do you not? Have you given a second thought to the chicken whose neck was wrung to provide your supper tonight?"

So coldly handsome—dark hair falling over the pale profile of some god sculpted by a Greek genius—who would have believed he could have been uttering such horrible words?

He broke off a spray of blossom from a nearby bush. "These flowers need only air and water—and yet they live. Do you ask the flowers why?" He tossed the spray away.

A slightly drunk couple, trying to keep lips together and to walk at the same time, were weaving from side to side along the path.

"I know that, in order to live, I must take life from a certain sort of being," he continued.

The cuddling pair ended their kiss with an explosive smack. The girl, scarcely older than Lucy, but with black

113

on her eyes, looked up at Ruthven, her paint-smeared mouth stretched in a welcoming grin, until her loving partner jerked her towards himself again. Heads together, they wandered into the shadows.

"Not that one," said Ruthven. "Any more than you would feast on rotten fruit or stinking fish. Why it must be a certain kind of being I question no more than you question why you prefer fresh bread to a moldy loaf."

As if in anticipation the tip of his tongue swept across his colorless lips, red against the white.

Sickness rose in my throat.

He went on, calmly, "The moon is full tonight. My appetite grows with the moon. It must be satisfied. You know what must happen." His usually even voice rose in a kind of great joy.

"Not if I can help it!" As I aimed a blow, he caught at my arm. Once again I felt my strength fade away. I could no more struggle against this thing than a puppet can defy its master.

"Surely you do not intend to test your strength against mine," he murmured. "You may excite admiration barefisted in the gymnasium, but I assure you twenty like you would never win against me.

"You have stopped me before. Can you guess the pain you caused me? The agony in Rome of appetite denied. You paid, though. I had to wait, so I waited—until I could strike at you. You paid for your interference with her life."

"Not Ianthe!" I cried.

"Ianthe," he breathed. "Accounts must always be settled. Now you will pay again. You tried to break your oath. For that you must be taught. This, dear Aubrey, will be your lesson. You know what must happen tonight. Indeed, I will make sure that you know every-

114

thing. But you will be unable to lift one finger to prevent it, or to whisper one word of warning.

"*Remember your oath.*"

I struggled. A rabbit might as well try to free itself from a trap.

"Go back," he said. A human might have spoken in contempt, but his emotions were not human. "Go back to the place you came from. Now."

He released me.

I was determined not to accept his cursed dictation mildly. My feet dragged slowly, as though I were leaning my weight against a gale, all the way back to the pavilion. On the surface the party seemed to have progressed gaily enough in my absence. Sir George was ordering more champagne.

"And when shall we have the fireworks?" he called after the waiter.

"Werry soon, sir," the waiter called back. "Werry soon."

I staggered up the steps and collapsed into a chair. Glances flashed from one to the other. Lady Loveborough raised an eyebrow and continued a conversation with Lucy as though nothing had happened. Lucy's eyes were troubled on my account.

I began to tell them that there was no need to worry; that I had merely been taking a brisk walk to keep off a possible headache. This was true enough, because my head was ringing as though it had been squeezed by a giant fist. I stopped as soon as I realized my words were slurred.

Jane smiled and rested a sympathetic hand on my arm. Gentle though her touch may have been, on the spot which Ruthven's fingers had just bruised it was too much. Involuntarily my arm jerked away.

Jane's smile froze. She turned it and her understanding brown eyes to Captain Beverley on her other side. Something suspiciously like a tear shone in Lucy's eye. Max winked. They all believed I was drunk.

The situation was not unheard-of, and Sir George was prepared to make allowances for my being young. I was even served with another glass of wine.

On the rotunda the fiddlers were joined by a ballad singer, who gave way to a juggler, and then to an expert in magic tricks. A touch of magic came back to the evening for everyone except me.

Slowly the heaviness that troubled me lifted. Half-smiles greeted one or two of my remarks—but they were not what I wanted to say.

I pressed my burning forehead against one of the gilded pillars, until I realized that this might be taken as further evidence of my over-indulgence. A low railing surrounded the pavilion. I held on to this to disguise the shaking of my hand, even though it might look as though I was using it for support.

"Unless the fireworks start soon," protested Max, "I will sing a comic song by way of entertainment."

I began to talk—partly to prove that I was still capable of speech, and partly to quiet those warning voices inside my head.

"Any moment now a girl will die," they were saying. "A girl. At any moment. Is to die."

Ruthven passed by. Deliberately—as he had threatened. I must know everything.

No one else in our party saw him. Miss Arabella Wynter was preoccupied with Augustus Snoad, and the eyes of all the others were fixed on me.

A girl walked close to Ruthven—not with him but a pace or two behind, as though she were on an invisible leash. Her blank face, measured step and unseeing eyes gave her the appearance of a sleep walker.

I recognized the blue muslin and lacy shawl. She was the girl we had noticed with her family at the start of the evening. There would be no need for Ruthven to tear that dress; her young, white throat was already exposed.

I realized then that everyone, even Arabella and Snoad, was waiting expectantly. I had paused in mid-sentence, hand in the air like a statue. I could not remember what I had been about to say.

After turning up the path towards the arbor of our previous meeting Ruthven was swallowed by the dark-ness, and the girl with him.

Still my audience waited. Still I neither moved nor spoke. When would the screams proclaim that the beast's foul appetite was again being satisfied?

I was the one to scream.

"No!" I howled. The table beside me went over with a crash of broken glass as I jumped over the pavilion railing.

I was still shrieking "No, no, no," as I ran down the dim paths; not even hearing the protests as I pushed aside anybody in my way.

Disregarding elderly couples, pairs in love, solitary walkers, I raced down the leafy tunnels, past the grottos, under the dancing lights until I reached the arbor.

Ruthven was there with the girl. She could not hear me, partly because of her seeming trance, partly because my voice had dwindled to a hoarse croak. Ruthven was savoring the moment, all the more precious to him because he knew that I was there—unable to help her, unable to attack him.

Then an idea flashed across my mind. I could not touch him, but I might attack her. He was already lifting

117

the scarf from her shoulders. His head was tilted, his mouth slightly open.

His laugh was like a signal. Leaping across the arbor, I hurled myself at the girl and the pair of us crashed to the sanded, wooden floor.

The girl began to scream, but these were screams of outraged dignity, not the last despairing cries they might have been. I did my best to keep myself between her and the monster towering over us. Not for long.

I was picked up bodily and hurled into a box hedge on the other side of the path.

I had the impression of all this happening very slowly, giving me time to reflect even before I hit the bush. Would he once again try to choke the life out of me? Or would he take her first?

He did neither. As I disentangled myself from the twigs, I heard the gabble of many voices and a pounding of feet, even above the girl's continual squealing. Ruthven was gone. The girl and I faced the encircling crowd.

It was a crowd in an ugly mood. The girl accused me of making violent advances, brutal assault and tearing her shawl. The least I might expect was a ducking in the ornamental lake.

At that moment Sir George arrived with all the dignity of an admiral's flagship, and the rest of our party behind him. The crowd recognized in him a person of authority. Complaints were addressed to him with the insistence that something should be done about me.

Sir George raised an impressive hand. "The young man is clearly drunk," he boomed. "I shall take him into my charge."

One or two in the crowd gave a faint, ironic cheer.

My head felt curiously light, almost like a balloon

ready to float away. Perhaps I was a little drunk after all. Or perhaps this was a relief after so prolonged a strain. At the back of my mind a warning echo repeated, "Accounts must always be settled. Always." Well, that was something to be settled later.

I turned to my party and tried to look cheerful. There was Sir George, beside whose complexion the brightest Chinese lantern paled. There was Lady Loveborough, mentally removing me from her list of eligible bachelors. There was Captain Beverley, wondering whether this might all have been a plot to throw him into the arms of Miss Loveborough. There was Miss Wynter, still giggling behind her fan. There was Lucy, whose obvious distress at my seeming offense I longed to soothe away.

Behind Lucy stood Ruthven.

He said nothing. Not a muscle of his face moved. He stood, as always, pale and still. His very presence brought its own message: "Here is the price you will now pay."

No one else saw him. No one else was looking that way. I wanted to tell them about that fiend standing there. That he should not be allowed to escape again to create more havoc.

An evil smile flickered across his lips as I opened my mouth, trying to force out words. Something of the agony of my efforts must have been picked up by the crowd, because I heard mutterings.

" 'Avin' a fit."

"Not responsible."

"Put 'im away for 'is own good."

Trying to raise my hand was like trying to lift the greatest weight I had ever imagined. Then I realized that the answer lay not in mere muscle, but in strength of will. Concentrating all my resolution, I imagined my hand rising. Slowly it obeyed, my accusing finger pointing.

"He—he . . .," I managed to gasp.

The fireworks exploded at last. The most brilliant of all were inside my head.

The rest I forget.

SEVENTEEN
What Was the Message?

The following weeks were filled with confusion. Familiar streets became outlandish and threatening. I would lose my way, forget my name, be brought home by strangers. I knew I had received some terrible warning, but could not remember what it was or who it was intended for.

Some things I do remember from that time . . .

I remember Lucy pleading with my guardian until he, poor man, not knowing which way to turn, tore off his wig and threw it at me, shouting, "You are driving me as mad as he is."

I remember being locked in my room in darkness, heavy curtains drawn.

I remember leaving my guardian's house through the window and over the rooftops.

I remember the room again with heavy iron bars at the windows.

All this time, weighing on my mind, was that urgent message I had forgotten to deliver . . .

I remember Lucy sitting by my side, reading to me, and my confusion becoming less painful.

I remember the coach journey with Lucy still by my side, on our way back to our home in Leicestershire . . .

* * *

Suddenly the corn in our fields had ripened, the summer sun blazed triumphantly, and I felt well again. A pity I could not remember that message, but after so long it could hardly matter.

One day, as I sprawled on the grass, an old straw hat on my head and the covers of *The Ancient Mariner* curling at my side, sunbonneted Lucy brought out a stool, and sat as sedately as ever in front of me.

"Are you sure you are quite well now, dear Aubrey?"

"Item one, I have never been ill," I replied. "Item two, I have never been better. Why do you ask?"

"Because if what I say should distress you, I would never forgive myself."

I put my hands on her shoulders and looked into her eyes.

"Lucy, my dear, we have always been direct and honest with each other. Oh, sometimes I have been thoughtless, thinking only of myself; but at least I am honest enough to admit even that. If the time should come when we could not tell the truth to each other, the world would be in a sorry state indeed. Now tell me, with no beating about the bush, what is on your mind."

She considered for a few more seconds, then said solemnly, "I have had a letter."

"Bravo!" I clapped my hands. "My congratulations to the mail coach. And what does your letter say?"

She took a breath. "He has asked me to marry him."

Reapers moved slowly along a field beyond the park. At last I feared my silence might be taken for disapproval.

"I am happy for you, my dear," I said. "But why not tell me sooner?"

"You seemed so contented. I did not wish to shatter your peace of mind."

"All that could do such a thing now, dear Lucy,

would be your unhappiness. Now, please tell me all. Who is he?"

"The Earl of Marsden," she said, biting her lip as though embarrassed by the title.

"An earl, no less," I laughed. "You carried him off under the noses of Miss Amelia, Miss Arabella and Miss Jane. What will Lady Wynter and Lady Loveborough think when they hear of your conquest?"

"I imagine they have guessed already. Before we left London Lady Loveborough insisted that she should take care of all the arrangements."

"So advanced already? Perhaps you ought to explain how all this came about."

"He called to ask after you when he learned you were ill. At first he was not admitted. No one was. However, he called again and again. He was most anxious—and so very sympathetic. That way we saw each other regularly.

"At last he confessed that he called as much to see me as to inquire about you. Just before we came back to the country he proposed. We agreed that nothing more could be done until you were quite well."

"But I have been well for a long time, and still you did not mention him."

"I was afraid he may have proposed in haste, and be repenting at leisure. I heard no more from him—until this."

She handed to me a sheet of crested paper. I half-recognized the writing, but could not exactly place the penman. The letter was signed "Marsden."

"I don't remember an Earl of Marsden," I said. "Why should he ask after me?"

"Perhaps you knew him under another name," she suggested. "He has only just come into the title. An elder brother died suddenly. He is connected with the diplomatic service. Do you suppose he could be one of Loveborough's friends?"

I patted her cheek. "Bless you. I doubt whether any of Loveborough's frie.. .s have the brains to belong to the diplomatic service."

"Now you understand why everything must be done so terribly quickly." Those serious blue eyes looked earnestly into mine.

"Why?"

"It is all in the letter. He has been offered an important embassy. He must leave in three days' time."

"Three days?" I scrambled to my feet, losing my straw hat in the process.

"We must be married before then, or wait until his return. He says it must be a choice between three days or three years. Dear Aubrey, I will say no if you want me to."

"Do you love him?"

"Love him? I am not sure what love is. I only know that when I am with him, I feel that I can deny him nothing."

"In which case, the sooner you are married to him, the better. But—three days! Is it possible to arrange a wedding in three days?"

"He has a special licence from the bishop."

"Connections with a bishop, too? Am I the only one not to know this man?"

"But I am sure you do—even if it is by another name. And our guardian was very taken with him. They have met. Our guardian declares he could not want better for me if I were his own daughter. He made very careful inquiries before giving his consent—and then only after seeing Marsden with his own eyes."

"Then he must be financially sound," I said. "And if our guardian agrees, who am I to say no? You will be happy, dear one. This man must make you happy. If he does not, he will have to settle accounts with me."

"Thank you, dear Aubrey." She threw her arms around my neck and kissed me. "Now I must write to him."

"You will do no such thing. You must pack at once. Only three days? We must be in London before any mail coach. There is so much to be done. Do you suppose Lady Loveborough is waiting with the wedding dress in her hands?"

Lucy laughed so rarely, it did my heart good to see her now. Raising her petticoats like a little girl, she raced across the grass to the house. She had left her precious letter in my hand.

I did not recognize the crest. In spite of the cloudless sky a shadow seemed to fall across the page. Although the landscape around me was bathed in golden light, I shivered. Someone must have been walking over my grave.

As I approached the house, I heard the domestic staff in turmoil. Packing had begun.

In spite of heroic efforts, the task was not completed until after nightfall. We decided that, by starting at daybreak, with frequent changes of horses, we might arrive in London by bedtime. We accomplished this, though barely.

As we approached London, a harvest moon hung like a great balloon low in the sky. The horses, sensing they were nearing journey's end, picked up speed. Lucy, who had been sleeping with her head on my shoulder, stirred.

"How bright it is," she exclaimed.

"Full moon."

"Not quite," she corrected me. "It will not be truly full until the night after tomorrow."

"By then you will have been Lady Marsden for several hours."

"How difficult that is to believe."

"Stranger things have happened," I joked. Then shivered again.

At once she was all concern, thinking I had caught a cold. I could not tell her that I was bothered by a half-forgotten memory. Instead I wagered that I should be in bed at our guardian's house before she finished her explanations to Lady Loveborough.

EIGHTEEN
Deadly Wedding

Although I retired to bed with a generous portion of my guardian's best wine inside me, I had difficulty in sleeping.

Perhaps I was overtired. Perhaps I was dazzled by the harvest moon shining through the bars over my window —hateful bars: no need for them. Perhaps it was something my guardian had said.

I had been looking forward to meeting Marsden the next day, only to be told that would be impossible. He was away settling affairs at his estate before his long absence at the embassy in Transylvania. I should meet him soon enough.

"A fine figure of a man, though," my guardian said. "Puts me in mind of—what's that poet fellow?— Byron."

Why should I feel that something forgotten was trying to force its way to the surface of my mind?

On the morning of the wedding, I joined my guardian for breakfast at six o'clock, although my appetite could not cope with the chops and dark beer his manservant, Roberts, set in front of me. By half past eight we were bathed, shaved and dressed in our best.

I tossed aside two crumpled ties before my fumbling fingers had tied one to my satisfaction.

Could I be worrying about the speech I would be expected to make? It would be brief and I was sure I could make the quests laugh with the story of my offer

of English pistols as a wedding present. The offer had
been greeted with laughter, in spite of my pointing out
that I had in mind protection in the wilder parts of
Europe rather than pistols for two on the wedding night.

I joined my guardian in his study. In honor of the
occasion he had taken his best flowered vest out of moth
balls, and changed his everyday wig for one of brighter-
colored rust.

For the next half hour we paced up and down, my
guardian sniffing and tutting, myself starting sentences,
then forgetting what I was about to say.

What was wrong with my memory? Why had so
much become lost? The waiting did not help, and there
was nothing more to do until Marsden's carriage arrived.

The city clocks were striking nine when we heard his
horses outside. Roberts showed him up at once, throwing open the door and making the announcement as
though introducing guests at an ambassador's ball.

"The Earl of Marsden, sir."

Was it customary for a bridegroom, no matter how
tall and elegant, to wear nothing but black and white on
his wedding day?

Was his lordship also nervous? For he was as pale as a
corpse, with a lock of black hair falling across his white
forehead. His dark gray eyes, on the other hand, were as
lively as burning coals. Where had I seen such eyes
before?

"I perceive you do not recognize me, Mr. Aubrey," he
remarked.

"I—I feel I should," I stammered. "But your lordship
has the advantage."

"Then I must stir your memory," he said. "A man
really should be aware of whom his sister is about to
marry."

He laughed. The low, evil laugh of some devilish creature committing some monstrous act, and enjoying it.

With that reminder, recollections swarmed back into my mind with all the pain of a thousand stings. Of course I knew him.

This was Ruthven.

A shudder of pain seemed to split my skull. While the brief agony lasted, I clutched at my head and shut my eyes.

At my elbow I could hear my guardian clucking a bewildered mixture of apology and sympathy. When the red mist lifted and I could see again, nothing had changed outwardly. Ruthven still stood in the doorway, his lips curved in a malignant smile. I had robbed him of his prey and this was his exquisite revenge. His next victim was to be Lucy.

"What is the matter, my boy?" whispered my guardian anxiously. "A touch of the old trouble?"

I did not answer. I could not answer. I could not speak.

Then I had Ruthven's neck in my hands, squeezing with all my might, while someone in the room was screeching like a maniac. It was myself.

Ruthven did not resist, but waited patiently as my guardian and Roberts pulled me away, hanging on to my arms.

Alerted by the hullabaloo, other servants rushed up the stairs. In my present frenzy I could have shaken off every one of them. If only Ruthven's eyes had not been upon me!

Those eyes numbed a man's will and turned his body into an unresponsive sack.

"You will submit," murmured the muted voice.

"Not again!" my guardian wailed. "Take him up to his room."

"You will go with them quietly," insisted Ruthven.

"The wedding!" cried the old housekeeper. "He'll miss the wedding."

"It is not essential that he should attend now," purred Ruthven. "After all, he knows exactly what his sister will be doing."

"Not a word of this attack to anybody," ordered my guardian. "You servants understand that? Can't have the wedding stopped. Now, for heaven's sake, lock him in. Thank goodness those windows are barred."

The servants did not need to hold or push me. When Ruthven commanded, I had no choice but to obey.

Behind me on the stairs the old housekeeper was weeping, "Poor Mr. Aubrey. He never tried to murder anybody before. This will mean the lunatic asylum for sure."

Below, my guardian was giving instructions to the coachman, "St. George's Church, and the quicker the better."

The door of my room was shut behind me and a key turned in the lock. Then came the sound of bolts being pushed home. I was as secure here as in the deepest dungeon of the Tower of London.

I crossed to the window and clutched at the bars. Above the roofs of the houses opposite I could see an expanse of blue sky. It would be a fine day for a wedding.

NINETEEN
Ten Hours to Moonrise

I lost track of time. Presumably everyone was now assembled at the church. Lucy was about to be given in the mockery of a marriage.

A bird flew past the window and perched on the chimney opposite. If only I had the freedom of that bird! Though a poor sort of freedom after all—prey to any hungry cat or boy with a gun.

My train of thought ran like a burning fuse from one idea to the next. From bird to boy. From gun to pistol. My pistols were in my traveling case. I knew now what to do.

I loaded one and merely primed the other. Then I beat on the door, calling for the servants.

Mrs. Henderson puffed up the stairs, plaintively coaxing me, "Do rest quiet, Mr. Aubrey. That noise don't do any good."

I pleaded with her to listen carefully to what I was about to say, for I would be able to say it only once. When I was sure I had her attention, I asked her to beg my guardian's forgiveness for what I was about to do. I intended to shoot myself.

"No, Mr. Aubrey," she cried. "You're not to do no such thing. Not on no account."

In reply, I fired the unloaded pistol, and followed this with as loud a groan as I could muster.

She began to call for the manservant. "Mr. Roberts. Oh, Mr. Roberts! Mr. Aubrey's a-dying!"

While Roberts answered her cries, I loaded the pistol—this time correctly, with a bullet.

There was a tap at the door, and the manservant asked fearfully, "Are you feeling all right, sir?"

I answered this with a noise which I hoped might be taken for a death rattle. Outside, the bolts were drawn, the key was turned and the door flung open.

With a pistol in either hand I faced the servants. The old man gasped: the old woman shrieked.

"Mr. Roberts. Mrs. Henderson," I greeted them. "I am indeed bitterly sorry for this discourtesy, but will you please to step inside?"

Not being inclined to argue with a fully armed lunatic, they did as I asked. I motioned them to the window while I edged towards the door. Finally I slipped through and shot the bolts.

"Please make yourselves comfortable," I shouted. "I am sure this will be the first room Mr. Armitage will make for on his return from the wedding."

The mere mention of the wedding reminded me that there was much to be done and no time to do it.

As well as time, I needed money. In the study I broke open my guardian's strongbox. If he preferred charges, this could even prove a hanging matter. I put my trust in his affection for me, but even if worst should come to the very worst, I had no choice. This had to be done for Lucy.

First, a taxi to St. George's, hoping that I might be in time to halt the ceremony. A puzzled porter in the empty church informed me that I was at least an hour too late.

I hired a coach and a pair of capable horses. I had expected more trouble over this, but discovered that sufficient money thrown down with a commanding manner works a magic of its own.

I had no idea how far in front of me Ruthven might be when I set off after him. At least there were no problems of direction. There was no mistaking the Dover Road.

I planned on changing horses at Rochester and Canterbury, and hoped that the stable boys, spurred by the promise of sufficient reward, might perform each turnabout with record speed.

Clocks were striking twelve as I clattered out of the city yard. Ten more hours of daylight. Could I cover that seventy-odd miles in the time? There was only one answer. I had to.

Ruthven's attacks on young women had all been made after dark. If this pattern was repeated, I had only until the sun went down.

At the first rest stop I learned that a carriage with a lord and a young lady had changed horses there. Like me they had not paused for refreshment.

"'Is lordship bein' 'opeful of reachin' Dover by nightfall," said the stableboy. "And 'avin' that particular young lady as passenger, I understands 'is lordship's 'urry. Blue eyes and 'air as gold as a guinea. 'Ow far ahead, sir? About 'arf an hour—give or take a minute."

I had to reduce that lead. My advantage lay in Ruthven's thinking me still under lock and key. He was merely in a hurry; I was desperate. Even if he arrived at Dover after dark, he could take his revenge at leisure. If I arrived even a few minutes after dark, I might well be too late.

At Canterbury, in the late afternoon, I learned that I had reduced the lead to a quarter of an hour. At the same time, I earned angry looks from the man in charge over the state of the horses. I heard him muttering to a stableboy about the ways of the upper class. Then he must have noticed what I had by my side, and gaped.

"Have you never seen pistols before?" I snapped, and was away again.

Fatigue was beginning to make its mark. My mouth was dry, my arms and back ached, my eyes were stinging with dust.

The blue of the sky deepened, overlaid with bars of red. By the time I reached the outskirts of Dover, the sun was below the horizon. A bat blundered past my head and squeaked away into the growing dusk. In one or two windows candlelight gleamed. How many minutes did I have? How far ahead was Ruthven now?

Stableboys were still dealing with his lordship's carriage as I reined in my pair in the yard. I leaped from the seat, shouting instructions.

Clutching a pistol under my coat, I ran into the parlor.

The inn walls were decorated with tools and trophies of the fishing trade, from a whaler's harpoon to a stuffed pike. Of human presence there was no sign.

Then, a freckled girl in a cap and apron, lamp in hand, carefully descended the stairs. Seeing me, she paused under a picture of fishermen catching salmon with lamp and spear.

She eyed me up and down as I asked if his lordship had arrived. I had time to take in every detail of the picture over her head before she slowly nodded.

"Which room?" I panted. "Quickly! This is a matter of life and death."

She pointed. "Top o' the stairs. Had I better let 'im know you're asking?"

"I can announce myself," I said, taking the flight two steps at a time.

A candle had been lit in Ruthven's room, the yellow of its flame turning the sky beyond the open window to deep purple and Lucy's hair to a tumble of gold. She was leaning slightly out of the window, breathing in the evening air.

Ruthven had taken off his coat. In his white shirt he presented a cool contrast to my travel-stained condition. His hands were on Lucy's shoulders.'

As the door latch clicked, he straightened. "Did I ring?" he asked, then realized who had entered.

There was silence until Lucy, sensing something wrong, turned and saw me.

"Aubrey!" she cried, and ran to me. "I wanted to come to you, but Marsden said there was no time."

Words still would not come. I could only nod.

"So you came to me instead," she went on. "How you must have ridden. Marsden drove our horses hard all the way. I had to beg him to spare the whip. Now you have come to bid us goodbye."

I shook my head.

"Why so quiet, dear Aubrey?" she asked, taking my arm. "Cannot you speak?"

Again I shook my head. There was only one thing of which I wished to speak, and that was forbidden by a power I could not defy.

"You may speak to me," murmured Ruthven. "I give you leave. Why are you here?"

"To kill you," I said.

Lucy gasped. I wanted to explain to her but the diabolical power still held.

"That pistol is primed and loaded for the purpose, I presume?" Ruthven's superior smile was now a sneer.

"Yes."

"Foolish young man. Why would you wish to shoot me? So that Lucy should not go the way of the others?"

"The—others?" Lucy began to interrupt.

"Be quiet, my dear," insisted Ruthven, gently, but firmly.

"But, Marsden . . ."

"You will not speak again until I wish you to speak."

"I—I . . ."

"You—will—not—speak."

Lucy was silent.

"My dear Aubrey, do you suppose I will now be content with a mere girl's life? Even this girl's life? Oh, no. I am demanding a greater payment. Your sister is now my bride. According to the words of the ceremony, we are one. Whatever I am, she will become. When that transformation is complete, when she too sucks the life from her victim's neck, when, in short, she has become that thing you detest—a vampire—only then shall I consider our account balanced. What a pity you will not be alive to see it, but at least you know what is to happen."

"Never!" I cried. "I would rather kill her myself."

"I think you will not," said Ruthven. "The toy you carry holds only one shot. For her—or for me? I say neither. It is for yourself."

While he was speaking, his eyes were fixed on mine. Two dark eyes in a dead white face.

"You will do it now," said that voice. "You will shoot yourself."

I tried to avoid those eyes, but they came closer and closer until they seemed to fill my world.

"Now," he mocked. "You have never scored a bull's-eye in your life. You could not possibly miss now. A bull's-eye, then. Hit the bull's-eye."

His eyes were like two black spots.

"Shoot. Now! The bull's-eye."

I raised my pistol and fired.

Ruthven's face became a mask of blood as he staggered back against the table. The candle went out as it hit the floor and rolled across the room, coming to rest in front of the fireplace.

Ruthven did not fall. Instead his outstretched hands reached for me.

I had time only to gasp "Save yourself!" to Lucy before a grip like a trap fastened on my throat and I was struggling for breath.

Ruthven's pale face, close to mine, now seemed to have three dark eyes—blood streaming from the one in the middle of his forehead.

In the half-light, even as my sight began to dim, I could see that he was still smiling.

Suddenly he coughed and the pressure on my windpipe relaxed. He turned away from me.

As I leaned, gasping, against the window frame, I realized that something was sticking in his back. It was a fisherman's spear that Lucy had snatched from the wall near the fireplace in a pathetic attempt to help me. I doubt if the strongest man could have done much damage with it, much less a slip of a girl.

Lucy shrank back against the fireplace. The vampire laughed as he advanced on her. Desperately she pushed at him.

I am still not exactly sure what happened then. Perhaps Lucy caught him off balance, unawares. Perhaps his foot slipped on the candle we later found lying on the hearth. I only know that he fell backwards.

And that expression of devilish glee became a shriek like a soul's in hell. As it died away, Ruthven lay still.

From his chest protruded the head of the spear. In his fall it had been driven clean through his heart.

Across the room in the twilight I could just see the shine of Lucy's hair. Her voice had now returned. She had not screamed. Instead, she was making small whimpering sounds. I took her in my arms.

"Come," I whispered, and led her from the room.

Wanting to delay investigation as long as I could, I locked the door, and supported Lucy down the stairs. The slow girl was on her way up.

"A slight accident," I explained. "No need to clean up. His lordship is doing that. But the lady was alarmed. Get her a brandy, will you? And bring one for me, too."

The girl looked at me curiously, then went through to the kitchens. When had any lordship been known to clean up any mess? He would have rung for her.

She brought the brandy, though, as Lucy and I rested on a sofa in the parlor.

"I—I could not speak," gasped Lucy. "I tried, but—I could not."

"He was able to do that," I said.

"What did he mean—what I should become?" asked Lucy. "I don't understand."

I hugged her. "You will one day," I said. "There is so much to tell."

With his death I could talk about Ruthven again. Only now there was no time. Now a different danger threatened—from the law. With a dead body upstairs and a bullet from my pistol in his head, there was every chance that I would be arrested and tried. Even hanged.

Lucy understood. "He—he tried to kill you," she

said. "When questions are asked, I shall insist that was so."

"Drink your brandy, Lucy. Slowly."

We both drank brandy. Slowly.

Until the landlord stood in front of us. A heavily-built man, polite but firm, he was capable of dealing with any problem in running his inn. "Beggin' your pardon, sir, but the girl came to me wi' some mixed-up story about an accident." He picked up a lamp. "We wouldn't want his lordship to be put to any inconvenience. Shall us go up, sir?"

Lucy held my hand as we returned to the room with its awful secret. I unlocked the door.

While we had been downstairs, the harvest moon had risen, and was streaming through the open casement as bright as day.

There lay my pistol where I had dropped it. There lay a candle and stick from an overturned table. There lay an old fisherman's spear that should have been on the wall. In the patch of moonlight between the open window and the table lay—nothing!

Ruthven had gone.